Sierra Marshal

Cal Marsden, owner of the biggest spread in the territory, knew that Victor Gantry, his nearest neighbour, was a wanted man so he brought Steve Enders into the town of Anderson to arrest Gantry on a charge of murder and armed robbery. On the face of things, his actions showed a proper regard for law and order, but when Enders arrived in Anderson, it was soon apparent that Marsden had other reasons for wanting to see Gantry behind bars.

Discovering that Enders not only refused to arrest Gantry without further evidence, but also that the marshal was showing an unhealthy interest in his own activities, Marsden aimed to frame the lawman himself.

But Enders was no stranger to this kind of challenge and Marsden soon discovered that he had caught a wildcat by the tail, for the lawman knew a few tricks himself which finally forced a bloody showdown.

Sierra Marshal

Morgan Shaw

A Black Horse Western

ROBERT HALE · LONDON

© John Glasby 1964, 2003
First hardcover edition 2003
Originally published in paperback as
Sierra Marshal by Chuck Adams

ISBN 0 7090 7253 8

Robert Hale Limited
Clerkenwell House
Clerkenwell Green
London EC1R 0HT

The right of John Glasby to be identified as
author of this work has been asserted by him
in accordance with the Copyright, Designs and
Patents Act 1988.

All characters and events in this book are
fictitious and any resemblance to any real
person or circumstance is unintentional

Typeset by
Derek Doyle & Associates, Liverpool.
Printed and bound in Great Britain by
Antony Rowe Limited, Wiltshire

CHAPTER I

THE KANSAN

The sun at high noon had turned the town of Anderson into a stifling furnace with little dust devils eddying along the main street, covering the broad broadwalks with a thin layer of yellow-white dust. Outwardly, the small cow-town was drowsy and peaceful. A handful of palomino ponies stood tethered to the rail outside the saloon, heads drooping in the heat, and at intervals along the street, one or two of the local inhabitants of the town lounged in the shade of the low-roofed buildings.

The sheriff's office was the one brick building in a long line of wooden erections that contained stores, one of the four saloons of which Anderson boasted and the livery stables. Frank Blaine, the sheriff, sat in his shirt sleeves in the tall, high-backed chair behind the desk, sat and sweated and stared suspiciously at the man seated in the chair in front of him. Cal Marsden was one of the most powerful men in the territory, owned the Lazy Y spread outside of town and had a big interest in the three saloons on this side of the street as well as a big stake in the bank and the one hotel in town. The two men lounging against the wall on either side of the door were both Marsden's hired hands, their thick fingers brushing the butts of the guns riding low at their hips.

Marsden sat back in his chair, aware of the faint film of sweat that showed on the sheriff's brow and a sense of superiority went through him as he stared at the other man contemptuously. Blaine was the law in this town only so long as he, Marsden, decreed – and the other knew it.

Tapping a long forefinger on the edge of the desk, he said, thinly: 'I warned you that if you wouldn't do anythin' about that *hombre* Gantry, I'd take the law into my own hands. Well, that's exactly what I've done.'

'You ain't done anythin' foolish, Mister Marsden?' said the other softly. He rubbed his fingers along his stubbled chin. 'You go shootin' around on Gantry's spread and you'll have the whole bunch of his boys on your neck.'

Marsden laughed harshly and the men at the door took it up. Then the rancher sobered instantly. 'You know as well as I do that Gantry is a cold-blooded killer, that he's wanted for murder and armed robbery in Kansas. Mebbe he figgered that by comin' here and setting up a spread bordering mine, he could escape the noose that's waitin' for him. Mark you, I've got nothin' against a man just because of his past, but Gantry has been rustlin' my cattle for a year now, as well as claimin' the spring that rightly belongs to me.'

'He does have the title deed to the spring,' Blaine pointed out.

'Hell, whose side are you on?' roared Marsden. 'I say that water belongs to me and by heaven I mean to have it. Gantry's a wanted man and if you won't bring him in for trial then I—'

Blains shook his head wearily. 'You know I ain't got no jurisdiction over any crime committed in Kansas, Marsden,' he said tightly. 'You'll have to get a Kansas marshal for that job.'

Marsden sat forward in his chair, a pleased smile spreading over his face. 'Glad to hear you say that, Blaine,' he grinned, lips pulled back from his teeth like the snarl of a wild animal. 'Because that's exactly what I've done. There's a marshal riding in on the next stage into Anderson, reckon he ought to be here tomorrow sometime and when he gets here, I'll expect you to give him all the help he needs to bring in Gantry for trial.'

Blaine shrugged. 'Well,' he said quietly, 'I'll do that, of course. But don't blame me if things don't go exactly as you plan.'

'You reckon there's any reason why they shouldn't?' asked the other.

'Don't rightly know,' conceded the sheriff. 'But what d'you reckon Gantry will be doin' while you're gettin' ready to toss him in jail? If he's the sort of killer you say he is, I figger he'll fight.'

'All the better if he does,' declared Marsden, getting heavily to his feet. He stood looking down at the man in front of him and for the first time, he began to wonder about Frank Blaine. Was the other quite the fool, the coward, he had always taken him to be? It was possible that with a man like Gantry at the back of him to stiffen his courage a little, Blaine might even turn against him. The thought worried him for a moment, then he thrust it out of his mind. He had nothing to fear from the sheriff and even if the other did go over to Gantry before the marshal came, none of the townsfolk would go with him. He could rely on their support if it was needed against Gantry.

He was feeling well pleased with himself as he left the Sheriff's office, swung up into the saddle and rode out of town with his two men riding closely behind him. Heat followed them along the narrow, dusty trail and the hoofs of their mounts stirred up more of the throat-clogging dust so that it swirled about them in a thick, yellow cloud.

Three miles passed under their horses and then they topped a low rise and rode down the winding trail where it ran between two spreads. Marsden reined his mount on a low knoll, stared over the flat ground that lay to the west with a look of hatred, blended with triumph in his bleak, grey eyes. Very soon, that land and its precious water would be his. Once Gantry was out of the way, safely locked up in the jail in Anderson, he would be able to put his plans into action. A lynch mob could be formed quite simply inside one of the saloons after feeding them plenty of whiskey and once Gantry was dangling from the end of a rope, there would be nothing to stand in his way. There had been talk of a daughter who was now somewhere back East, but it seemed unlikely that any woman would try to run a ranch here. Anyway, he would have his hands on everything long before she managed to get here, if she heard of her father's death.

Then, abruptly, all thought of this fled from his mind. The sun was just beginning to drift down towards the west and the lengthening shadows played over the small stream that officially marked the boundary of his spread. Less than a quarter of a mile on the other side of the stream lay the well which he claimed was his. Now, he noticed, there were five bleak-faced men lying sprawled in the shade of the small clump of trees overlooking the stream, with a newly-built fire burning on the bank.

Marsden ran a dry tongue over his lips. The men down there didn't look like any of Gantry's hired hands, but there was no sense in taking any chances; and one thing was sure, they were trespassing on his land. He loosened the gun in his holster, glanced sideways at the two men with him, then gave a little nod of his head. They walked their mounts soundlessly down to the far side of the slope, reined in when they were less than twenty feet from the men.

'Seems to me you men shore picked the wrong place to make camp,' he said thinly. As they jerked around, three Colts were lined on them, freezing any movement they may have made.

'This your place, mister?' asked one of them sullenly.

'That's right,' said Marsden, tight-lipped. 'and I'm mighty particular about who camps on it.'

'Ain't meanin' no harm,' growled another of the men. His eyes flicked towards the horses which had been tethered by the stream, a few yards away. 'We was jest ridin' through when we spotted this stream.'

Marsden regarded them dubiously. He recognised the type clearly. Ruthless killers, probably on the run from the law, yet willing to sell their guns to the highest bidder. His voice was cold and irritable as he asked: 'Where are you *hombres* from?'

The tall, black-bearded man who seemed to be the leader of the bunch, said thinly: 'We rode through Chester a coupla days ago. Up from Kansas.'

Marsden nodded, suddenly thoughtful. 'You say you're from Kansas. Know anythin' of a man called Enders, Steve Enders?'

He saw the sudden gust of expression that passed over the other's features, saw the tensing of the muscles under the dark skin, the way the men glanced at each other tightly.

For a second, the big man's face was purple, then he said softly, but with a touch of menace: 'You a friend of that marshal's, mister?'

Marsden shook his head. 'I've hired him to do a little job for me, but that don't make him my friend.'

The others were still wary. A plan was beginning to form in Marsden's mind, but at the moment he wasn't quite sure of it. He reckoned that if it ever did come to a showdown between Gantry and himself, if something did go wrong and there was no lynching, he would need every man who could use a gun on his side; and he didn't want these men, who were so obviously of that kind, going over to Gantry, if he frightened them off his land.

With an insolently wise look, the ruffian said: 'We saw

9

Enders back in Chester when we rode out. He took the stage for Anderson.'

'That's what I figgered,' nodded Marsden slowly. 'Any other passengers?

'Another *hombre* and a girl,' said one of the others.

'A girl.' Marsden pricked up his ears at that, a little thought running through his mind. 'You know who she was?'

The leader shook his head, but one of the other men spoke up. 'I did hear the driver call her Miss Gantry,' he said.

Gantry! That complicated things. If the girl came here, it could mean a lot more trouble for him. He let his thoughts twist around in his head for a moment, then regarded the outlaw bunch in front of him speculatively.

'You men looking for a job?' he asked abruptly.

The tall man's eyes narrowed to mere slits and there was a craftly look on his face. 'If I heard you right, mister,' he said thickly, 'you're bringing in that Kansas marshal to do some work for you. You wouldn't be thinkin' of turnin' us over to the law, would you?'

'What your past is, matters nothin' to me,' snapped Marsden. 'It could make things difficult for me if that girl you saw gettin' onto the stage in Chester should get here alive.'

The black-bearded outlaw gave a harsh laugh. 'You askin' us to bushwhack a woman, mister?'

Marsden let his glance range over the men clustered around the fire. 'I reckon it won't be the first time,' he muttered coldly. 'Besides, it could be quite profitable to you.' He shrugged, still keeping the Colt pointed at the men. 'You could hold up that stage and in the fracas there could be a very regrettable accident.'

'And if this *hombre* Enders decides to start anythin'?' asked the other pointedly.

Marsden pondered that for a moment, then grinned viciously. 'I reckon that if he was to get shot too, it might make things even better for me. Nobody will recognise any of you men and there ain't no way they could connect you with me. Most of the townsfolk know that I've asked Enders to ride in and arrest this *hombre* Gantry on a charge of murder down in Kansas and it could easily be made to look like he arranged the killin' of the marshal. Then the sheriff in Anderson would be forced to act.' He nodded, as if pleased with the idea.

The ugly, black-bearded man moved away from the fire, glanced at the men with him. Marsden could see that the idea appealed to them also. Born killers, utterly ruthless, riding just one jump ahead of the law most of the time, hunted and hounded from one state to another, another two killings would make little difference to them.

The tall man turned, regarded him closely. 'Reckon we'll accept that proposition, mister,' he said shortly. 'Jest one thing. Anythin' we find on that stage, we take.'

'That's all right by me,' Marsden nodded. He threw a quick glance at the sky as he holstered his gun, motioning to the two men with him to do the same. 'I figger you'd better ride out now if you want to get that stage before they get in sight of Anderson.'

'Sure thing.' The big man nodded, turned and kicked out the fire with his boot, spewing the sand over it. Saddling up, the men paused for a moment, eyeing Marsden shrewdly, 'We'll take care of Enders and the girl,' grunted the other. 'But we may come ridin' back this way when we've got that cleaned up.'

'Any time, boys.' Marsden nodded. 'I reckon I could do with a few more men who can handle guns, and while you're on my payroll, there aint nothin' to fear from the law. Sheriff Blaine in Anderson does exactly as I tell him.'

The other scratched his ear thoughtfully, then wheeled his mount, said something to the men with him and they spurred their mounts cruelly, breaking them into a hard run that lifted the yellow-white dust around them, half hiding them from view as they rode over the hill, around a bend in the trail.

Marsden stared after them, then glanced back at the dying embers of the fire, a faint smile of triumph on his hard, bleak features. Silvers, the foreman, said quietly: 'You reckon you can trust those *hombres* boss?'

Marsden nodded. 'They'll do what I told them,' he said affirmatively. 'I know their type. It don't matter to them who they kill, so long as there's somethin' in it for them.'

Clem Norton brought the stage down the long, twisting road from the pass high in the hills, towards the flat, rolling plains which stretched out in front of them at the bottom of the stony incline. Dusk was creeping over the land now that the sun was touching the pine ridges behind them and their shadows fled long in front of them. Outlines of the land which had been sharp and easily discernible a little while before, had become softened by the growing darkness, losing both shape and form before encroaching night. Still, there was plenty of light for him to see by and very soon, the moon would rise and light the trail all the way into Anderson. He dug deep into the pocket of his jacket, pulled out the large, gold timepiece which had been a constant companion of his for more than forty years as driver of the stage. In the whole of that time, it had stopped only once and was never more than a minute behind the right time. According to the watch they were only ten minutes behind schedule, all due to a landslide back in the hills which had partly blocked the trail through one of the deep canyons cut in the rock and he had been forced to edge the stage slowly and carefully past the fallen rock and debris.

He leaned back on the hard, wooden seat, pulled a plug of tobacco from his pocket, bit hard on the end and wrenched off a chew with a powerful twist of his neck and jaw muscles. His teeth chewed ruminatively on the tobacco as he eased the downward plunge of the four horses, guiding them around the ragged outcrops of rock that jutted from the sides of the canyon wall. Once they reached the smooth trail across the plain, they would be able to pick up a little of the time they had lost in the mountains, he reflected.

He lifted his head, glanced about him in the gathering dusk. Far away to his right, beyond the rim of the high-walled canyon through which they were passing, where the last, undulating roll of the hills finally petered out, the smooth rangeland showed clearly even in the dimness. This was the border of the real cattle country, a land of powerful men holding vast areas of grassland, holding them against any intruders from the east, the settlers who were beginning to come here in greater numbers with every passing year. Clem spat a squirt of juice into the brush that bordered the canyon and scowled a little. He had no real liking for the cattlemen, but he reckoned that the open prairie ought to be free, free for a man to ride the trails to anywhere without having to come up against wire strung across it. Better the devil he knew, than the one he didn't.

He thought back to the three passengers he had picked up in Chester two days before. A queer bunch, he thought inwardly. The girl was pretty enough, but what would a woman like that be doing out here in this frontier country? Unless she was one of the rancher's daughters, coming back from schooling in the East.

Then there was that thin-faced *hombre*, crafty-eyed, who hung onto that black bag he carried as if there was a fortune in gold in it and he expected to have it taken from him at any moment. A gambler? Maybe. He shrugged and thought about the third member of the trio. He wasn't quite able to make up his mind about that one. He could be a lawman, or an outlaw. Either way, he looked as though he knew how to handle the two guns he carried. A strange mixture altogether.

Inside the stage, Steve Enders glanced idly out of the window into the darkening night. The journey from

13

Chester had been uneventful. They had spent the previous night at the way station on the edge of the desert beyond the mountains, resting up the horses before tackling the hard pull through the pass. He reckoned that they couldn't be far from Anderson now, noticed that they were beginning to pull out of the rough rocky canyon and beyond he could just make out the rolling rangeland.

He had been a little disturbed by the message he had received from Marsden. He did not know the man, yet the other claimed that his nearest neighbour, a man named Gantry, was possibly some relative of the girl who sat opposite him, her eyes closed, dozing a little. If Marsden was to be believed, then Gantry was a wanted man, a killer, a man accused also of armed robbery. Where Marsden had got this information he did not know and the other had not, as yet, enlightened him on that point. But as marshal, it was up to him to investigate anything like this, even if there turned out to be no truth in the accusation at all. It might be just a question of jealousy between these two men and Marsden was taking this way of getting his own back on the other. Evidently, Marsden had tried to get the sheriff in Anderson to arrest Gantry, but the other had refused to do so on the grounds that this case was outside of his jurisdiction, that it would need a Federal marshal to do the arresting. Strictly speaking, of course, that was correct. But Enders felt certain there was a little more to this than met the eye at a first glance. Certainly he intended to ask a few questions for himself before he arrested anybody.

The last red flames of sunset were dying in the west now and the rough stones, rattling under the wheels of the coach made an endless sound in his ears. He wondered how long it would be before they reached Anderson. There was the gnawing of hunger in his stomach and he spent a little time peering out into the darkness as he contemplated the meal he would eat once he got to the hotel there.

Bending forward, he eased his long body into a more

comfortable position, wished that these coaches had been built with better springs and it was at that moment that a rifle shot rang out from somewhere directly ahead of the stage. Somebody shouted a harsh challenge and there came an equally sharp defiant roar from the driver perched high on the seat. Then a fusillade of revolver shots broke out and through the window, Steve glimpsed the three men who came riding pell mell down the rocky slope, their horses sliding most of the way, forelegs held stiffly.

Without pausing to think, he grabbed the girl and thrust her down onto the floor of the swaying, jolting coach, aware of the frightened look in her wide eyes. For a second she struggled, newly wakened, and not divining his intention. Even as she lay there, Steve had pulled one of the Colts from its holster and was steadying himself behind the door, taking a snap shot at one of the men as the driver urged the horses forward with a sudden high-pitched yell. The stage bounced from one side of the trail to the other, but Steve's aim had been true in spite of the rough motion and the man dropped from his saddle and pitched to the rocks in front of his mount, his body rolling down the slope until it came to rest on the trail somewhere behind the fast-rolling stage.

Then another rider came leaping off the slope in a wild flurry of hoofs and broken brush. Steve had a split second view of a tall, black-bearded man with his hair blowing wildly about his face and a horse poised incredibly in mid-air and then horse and rider had hit the trail, miraculously remaining upright in spite of that bone-jarring impact.

He aimed a second shot at the rider, but missed. Then more gunfire broke out from the other side of the trail and Steve distinctly heard a coughing moan from the driver. Glancing up through the small opening in the roof of the stage, he saw that the other had slumped sideways, the reins dangling loosely in his nerveless fingers. One hand was up to his shoulder and as he swayed sideways with the jolting

15

motion of the coach, Steve saw the red stain on his shirt as the wind caught his jacket and blew it aside.

The horses pounding forward, ran out of control along the trail. Behind them, there came the unmistakable clatter of hoofs as the outlaws came behind them in pursuit.

'Stay down there,' he hissed to the girl as she turned a fear-filled face up to him. Glancing at the man in the corner, he said roughly: 'You got a gun, mister?'

The other shook his head tautly.

'Then you got one now,' Steve told him. 'And you'd better use it or you'll never get to Anderson alive.'

'But what are you going to do?' protested the other as Steve handed him one of his Colts.

'I'm going to try to get up there on the roof and stop this coach. If I don't, we'll be off the trail and turning over before we know where we are. Keep me covered with that gun.'

The other hesitated, lips twisting, then he turned and poked the gun out of the nearby window, firing it frantically at the oncoming men.

Steve paused for only a second. It was doubtful if the other would hit any of those men. His hands were trembling so much that even if the coach had been standing still, he would have missed, but he might be able to keep them from loosing off any shots at him while he clambered out onto the top of the swaying coach and got to those horses.

Thrusting the other Colt back into its holster, Steve twisted the handle of the door and pushed it open, hanging onto the upright just inside the coach with his other hand. The pull of air rushing past the stage almost tore his arm out of its socket. Grimly, he held on with a wrenching of neck muscles. The air screamed past his face, whipped his hair into his eyes, the dust lifted by the pounding hoofs of the horses getting into his throat and nostrils, choking and burning.

A bullet struck the side of the coach within an inch of his

hand and went ricocheting off into the distance with the shrill whine of tortured metal. Pulling air down into his lungs, he reached up with his hand, gripped the top of the coach and swung himself out of the open door. Rough edges of rock caught at him, cutting through his clothing, tearing his skin as the stage swayed precariously from side to side. There was a harsh pounding in his temples and a stab of pain in his chest as he began to pull himself up, thrusting his arms and legs to get a better grip. Once, he almost lost his hold and only a wild scrabbling with both hands enabled him to remain where he was. He glanced down for a moment at the rocky trail that flashed by under the stage. There was more shooting from behind him and glancing back along the trail, he saw that there were four men in the outlaw bunch, and that they were gaining rapidly on them. Gritting his teeth, he managed to swing his body onto the roof of the stage and lay for a moment, trying to get the breath back into his sorely bruised body where every movement of the coach sent stabs of agony through his body. It felt as if every rib in his chest had been broken by the bruising impacts. Bullets hummed like insects around him as he reached forward, gently eased the driver out of the seat and tugged the reins from his limp fingers. Savagely he hauled back on the leather, slackening the pace of the horses a little, guiding them around the last bend in the trial before they hit the bottom of the slope and came out onto the range.

Now they could have their head. The wheels spun crazily as they drove forward, kicking up a cloud of dust through which their pursuers were forced to ride. The black-coated man was still firing wildly from the window of the stage, but his shots were apparently having no effect. Turning quickly, confident now that the horses were under control, Steve eased the Colt from its holster and twisted in his seat, taking a quick aim at the men riding through the cloud of dust. One of the men swayed in the saddle as the slug took him in the shoulder, but he still remained upright, still came on.

There was something funny about this hold-up, Steve thought to himself. He vaguely recalled seeing that face which had belonged to the man who had leapt down out of the rocks onto the trail at their backs. Thinking back, he felt certain he had seen the other, and four men, back in Chester before they had ridden out and if that had been the case, then those outlaws would have known that the stage was carrying nothing of value, that the payroll which went from Chester to Anderson would leave two days later.

Yet they had attacked this stage and not waited for the other. It didn't make sense whichever way he looked at it, but there was no time now in which to try to think things out. The four killers were still on their trail and gradually lessening the distance between them.

He snapped another shot at them, then cursed softly as the hammer fell on an empty chamber. Moments later, there came the sharp bark of a smaller gun from almost directly below him. Glancing down, he felt a sense of surprise as he noticed the girl leaning from the window of the door through which he had earlier climbed. A quick glance told him that there had been nothing wrong with her aim as one of the men toppled sideways from the saddle and hit the dust, rolling for several yards before he lay still. The riderless horse swung off the trail and went racing off into the darkness.

Now the darkness was coming down fast and it was difficult to pick out the shapes of the riders closing in on them. He considered stopping the stage and making a fight for it, now that the odds had been evened a little, but the mere action of halting the running horses would expose him. He told himself that if the girl and the other man could keep on shooting, they might be able to stay ahead of them until they reached Anderson. It was doubtful if the others would continue to follow them into the town.

There was another angle that he was uncertain about. He

18

did not want to have all of these men killed. He wanted to know why this hold-up had been staged. It might be that Gantry had heard Marsden had sent for him and was determined to do anything to prevent him from getting into Anderson alive. Even as the thought passed through his mind, he dismissed it. That made no sense, for the other would surely know that his daughter would be travelling on the same stage and would certainly not want to expose her to danger or even death in a hold-up such as this. Then there had to be another angle, though he was damned if he could see what it was at the moment. But if they could wing one of these men, pick him up and force him to talk, then it might help to straighten out matters a lot.

Glancing ahead, he noticed the brush that grew up along the trail. It worried him a little. He would not be able to devote any attention to the men at his back while he was forced to guide the stage through that. He slashed at the horses with the long, bull-hide whip, felt them respond although they were tired from the long haul over the mountains. But he knew that they could not keep up this tremendous, heart-bursting pace much longer. They were tiring fast whereas the horses those outlaws were riding would undoubtedly be fresh.

A solitary shot hummed dangerously close to his ear as he bent low in his seat. Then, curiously, the firing died away. Glancing back in surprise, he saw that the three remaining men were spurring their mounts off the trail, cutting back in the direction of the mountains. With an effort, he reined in the plunging horses. The stage slid to a grinding halt as he applied the brake beside him.

Carefully, he eased the driver back in the seat, saw the stain on his shirt where the bullet had hit him in the fleshy part of the shoulder. The other opened his eyes as he moved him and the lips parted in a grimace of agony.

'Did we outrun 'em?' he said haltingly.

Steve nodded. 'We killed a couple of 'em, old-timer,' he

19

said quietly. 'Now just you lie back for a minute until I get you down inside the coach. Then we'll drive you into Anderson and get a doctor to take a look at that shoulder of yours. I reckon you'll not be driving this stage for a few weeks with a wound like that.'

'Shucks. It'll take more'n this flea-bite to stop me,' gritted the other. 'I been driving the stage for close on forty years now and I don't aim to let a little hole in my shoulder put me outa action.'

'All right then. But lie still and no more talkin'. You've lost a lot of blood and that slug will have to come out pretty soon.'

Looking down, he saw that the door of the stage had opened and the other two passengers had got out, and were peering up at him in the gloom.

'How bad is he hurt?' asked the thin-faced man, tautly.

'He's losing too much blood,' said Steve. He motioned to the other to come forward. 'Help me to get him down and into the stage. I'll drive the team the rest of the way into town. But we don't want to hang around here too long. Those critters may decide to come back.'

It was this thought, more than anything else, he thought wryly, that spurred the other into action. Together, they managed to get the driver onto one of the seats inside the coach where the girl pulled off his shirt and bandaged the wound with it.

Steve watched for a moment, then nodded in satisfaction. 'See what you can do for him until we reach Anderson, Miss,' he said quietly. 'And by the way, that was some fancy shootin' you did back there.'

'Thanks.' She did not look up, but continued with her task of strapping up the driver's shoulder. 'I learned to handle a gun when I was a little girl on the ranch. I guess that once you learn something like that, it isn't easily forgotten.'

'It certainly came in useful back there.' Steve waited for

another moment and then closed the door, climbed up onto the driver's seat, picked up the reins, and urged the tired mounts forward through the brush. Overhead, the sky was clear and dark and the first stars which had shown only dimly earlier were now shining with a bright, sharp radiance. Half an hour passed before the trail passed over a wide wooden bridge spanning a broad stream and a quarter of a mile further on, they rode into the town of Anderson, sprawling on both sides of the main street which ran as straight as a die from one side to the other.

Reining the horses to a halt in front of the stage office, Steve glanced down at the men who were waiting outside the low, wooden building. One of them pushed his way forward, stood with one hand on the door of the stage. The faint light from the window of the office caught the star he wore on his shirt.

'What happened, mister?' asked Sheriff Blaine harshly. 'Hold-up?'

'That's right, Sheriff.' Steve slid from the seat, dropping the reins over the backs of the team. 'Five men tried to stop us just as we were pulling down from the foothills. We killed two of 'em and the rest fled when we got out onto the rangeland.'

'What happened to Clem?'

'He's inside.' Steve jerked a thumb towards the stage. 'Hit in the shoulder. Better get him to a doctor right away.'

Blaine turned to one of the men near him. 'Fetch Doc Holdern,' he said tersely. Then he swung back on Steve. 'You recognise any of those men who tried to hold you up?'

'I saw them in Chester before we pulled out two days ago.'

Blaine's brows went up at that and he nodded thoughtfully. 'I reckon I'd better have a talk with you over in the office,' he said, then glanced up as the girl got out of the stage, followed by the black-clothed man. A momentary look of surprise guested over the sheriff's face, then he said evenly: 'Why, Miss Gantry. We weren't expectin' you to arrive back in Anderson. Your pa know you're here?'

'He's expecting me, Sheriff,' she said coldly. 'I understand from his letters that he's expecting trouble too. Seems somebody is trying to run him off his ranch.'

Blaine shrugged. 'Ain't heard nothin' about that, but I'll keep my ears open just in case. I wish your pa would come to me when he reckons there's somethin' like that goin' on. I'm supposed to be the law in these parts and if there's to be any feudin' and shootin', I want to know so I can stop it in time.'

'From what I've heard, you wouldn't stop it even if it were true.' The chill touch in the girl's voice was easily heard. 'Seems to me from what my father says that you're in cahoots with Marsden and if that's so, you ain't likely to be helping us.'

'Now you got no call to say such a thing,' protested the other shrilly. 'I do things as I see best and anybody who says I'm in cahoots with anyone in this town is a liar.'

But he was talking to himself, for the girl had turned and was walking off in the direction of the hotel further along the dark, quiet street. Steve made to follow her, but the sheriff said sharply, 'I said I wanted to talk to you, stranger. Where do you reckon you're goin'?'

'If you got no objections, I'd like to book a room at the hotel,' said Steve quietly.

The other hesitated, seemed to turn that over in his mind, his gaze travelling to the guns in the other's holsters and the way he held himself, loose and limber, as if ready for trouble. 'All right then,' he said finally, ungraciously, 'but I want to talk with you tonight, before you turn in.'

'You'll be Steve Enders,' said Blaine, looking up at the other from behind his desk.

Inside the small front office, the lamp on the desk threw long, twisting shadows around the room as the wick burned up and then dimmed. Steve eased his shoulders back against the chair, stretched out his long legs in front of him. Those two days in the cramped confines of the stage had cramped his limbs and he had not yet had a proper chance to stretch them, to get the blood working as it should.

'That's right,' he replied finally. 'I came in answer to a letter from Marsden. I gather he's one of the biggest ranchers in this territory. A pretty important man.'

Blaine gave a quick nod. 'He owns the Lazy Y spread, just outside the town. It borders Victor Gantry's place. There's always been bad blood between those two, mainly because of a well which is just inside Gantry's spread. Marsden claims that it belongs to him.'

'So he's determined to get rid of Gantry any way he can.'

'That's it, I guess.' The other got heavily to his feet, moved around the side of the desk and strode up and down the room, hands clasped behind his back. 'Marsden came to me a little while ago, wanted me to arrest Gantry on a charge of murder and armed robbery. He reckoned that Gantry was wanted in Kansas and it was my duty to bring him in. When I pointed out that I couldn't do that, he stormed out of my office. Yesterday, he came back and told me that he'd decided to take the law into his own hands, that he'd sent for somebody who could arrest Gantry and make the charges stick. I learned from him that it was you he had sent for and I expected you to be on the stage tonight.'

Steve nodded slowly. A little of the situation was beginning to make sense, but there were still several puzzling points about it that he did not fully understand.

'You got any idea who those *hombres* might have been who tried to hold up the stage tonight, Sheriff?'

Blaine stopped his pacing, then shook his head. 'None at all,' he said soberly. 'You got somethin' on your mind?'

'Just seems mighty peculiar to me that those men should attack this stage and not wait for the other coming along in two days' time, the one that will be bringing in the payroll. They must have known that there was nothing of value on this coach and yet they'd clearly laid a well-planned ambush for us. I reckon they were wanting something else than money or bullion.'

'What else is there that interests men like that?'

'Could be that Marsden had hired them to kill the girl. If he knew she was on that stage and that she could foil any plans he'd got, it's only natural that he'd want to make sure she didn't get into Anderson alive.'

Blaine's brows drew together into a hard, black line, then he shook his head. 'That don't make sense either,' he said shortly. 'Because Marsden must've known you would be on the stage too.'

'Yes, that's the one thing that's been worryin' me about this idea,' confessed Steve. He pursed his lips into a tight line. 'Somethin' here doesn't add up right. Mebbe I can get some of the answers when I have a talk with Marsden tomorrow.'

Blaine nodded his head slowly. His eyes shifted beadily over Steve's face, seeking for the smallest sign of what the other intended to do once he met up with Marsden. 'You still reckon that he may have had somethin' to do with this hold-up of the stage?'

'It could be,' Steve replied, a little curtly now. The other's manner was becoming patronising and Steve had no desire for a prolonged conversation with him, certainly not at this early hour of the morning, and after a two day ride in that stage. 'Now though, I'm goin' to get some sleep.'

'Of course! Well, I guess we'll run into each other in town and if there is anythin' I can do to help, I'll be only too glad to.'

Steve hesitated over his answer. He recalled what the girl had said when she had stepped off the stage and the thought still stayed in his mind in spite of the other's heated denial. He ought to tell the other of all the suspicions he had in his mind, but the sheriff's manner did not encourage him to disclose anything more about his future plans.

'I guess so,' he said quietly. Getting to his feet, he walked over to the door, opened it and stepped out into the street. Making his way along the boardwalk towards the hotel, he glanced back curiously. As he watched, the door of the sheriff's office opened. Blaine came cut and stood in the light of the lamp, looking about him almost furtively. Then he went back inside, and a moment later, the light went out as the other blew out the lamp and Steve saw the other's shadowed figure in the doorway, heard him lock it behind him, then saunter off in the other direction.

The lobby of the hotel was dark with brown wall panelling which only served to increase the gloom inside. There was a night clerk behind the desk. He glanced up from behind the paper he had been reading, then gave Steve a quick nod of recognition. Getting hastily to his feet, he took down the key to the room which Steve had ordered earlier and handed it over the desk to him. 'First floor,' he said quietly, pointing to the rickety stairs which led up from the other side of the lobby.

Taking the key, Steve climbed the creaking stairs wearily, unlocked the door of his room, went inside and, acting on impulse, locked the door behind him. He went over to the window, leaving the room deliberately in darkness. The street was clearly visible from his window and although yellow light still showed from some of the windows overlooking the boardwalks, the street itself appeared to be deserted. There was no sign of Sheriff Blaine.

Pulling off his jacket and shirt, he washed some of the dust off his body, then stretched himself out on the bed, staring up at the dimly-seen ceiling over his head, letting his thoughts run and coalesce in his head. There were evidently a host of things happening here about which he knew nothing; but he was determined to find out about them before he made any move. He had the impression that this man,

Marsden, was playing some deep game known only to himself and the thought worried Steve. He did not like working for a man if he knew very little about what the other was up to.

The moon had lifted from its early night position and threw a clear, frosty-silver glow over the town. It filtered in through the window and laid a pattern of light and shadow on the floor close to the bed. Downstairs. he heard some-one moving around softly, guessed that the clerk was still awake although it was unlikely there would be any other guests moving into the hotel that night.

Sleep deadened his senses and his eyelids drooped. When he awoke, it was dawn, there was a silver flush spreading over the tall hills to the east, touching the crests with a softness that would vanish and give way to a shimmering hardness once the heat had lifted during the morning. The clouds were just beginning to lose their painted look, becoming more solid as the red glow from the rising sun brightened and touched their undersides with flame.

Stretching, he went to the window, poured water from the tall pitcher into the basin, washed and shaved, felt better, and pulled on a clean shirt from his bag, putting it on before fastening the heavy gunbelt around his middle. Outside, the town was coming to life. A couple of riders rode by at a steady lope, heading out of town and a moment later, a wagon rattled from the direction of the livery stables and drew up outside the saloon.

Going down into the dining room, he chose a table opposite the door where he could watch everyone coming in. When the meal was brought to him by a swarthy, balding man he found it was far better than he had anticipated, well cooked and perfectly wholesome, fried eggs, sweet potatoes and three thick slices of ham. The bread seemed to have been freshly baked and there was hot coffee, as much as he could drink. He ate ravenously until he could eat no more, then sat back in his chair and rolled a smoke.

A moment later, the girl who had been on the stage the previous day came in and found a table near the door. She glanced across at him, smiled briefly in acknowledgement. He wondered inwardly what her attitude would be when she found out the real reason for his visit here, to arrest her father on Marsden's say-so. For the first time, he felt regret at what he was to do. Perhaps it might be possible to explain to her that this was no desire of his, then he put the thought out of his mind. He would have to ask a whole heap of questions yet, before he got to the bottom of the trouble here and when he did, it was just possible that things might turn out to be different from what he expected.

First, he would have to get himself a horse and a rifle, then he would ride out to the Lazy Y ranch and have a talk with Marsden, get his version of the story.

Finishing his smoke, he drank the last of the hot coffee, then pushed back his chair and got to his feet. The girl gave him a direct, almost challenging glance as he strode past her table, but said nothing. Outside in the street, he looked up and down the main street, then spotted the livery stables a few yards away. A man drifted out of the dimness at the back, eyed him curiously for a long moment.

'I'm lookin' for a good horse,' Steve told him. 'Got one for sale?'

'Could be,' murmured the other non-committally. 'You got money to pay?'

Steve took out the roll of bills from his pocket, nodded. The hostler glanced at them, eyes bright-hard, then led the way towards the stalls at the rear of the building. 'Got two mounts for sale,' he said harshly, 'You can take your pick.'

Steve looked them over and finally chose the tall black stallion. The hostler gave him an appraising look. 'He's a mean critter, mister,' he said warningly. 'I reckon he ,was brung up wild on the range and he's been only half-broke.'

'Reckon he'll suit me,' Steve said. 'Can you throw in a bridle and saddle?'

'Sure thing.' The other went into one of the empty stalls and came out with the saddle and bridle, watched while Steve threw them over the stallion, talking all the while in a soothing tone as the big horse skitted and pawed the ground.

Finally, he swung himself up into the saddle, glanced down at the hostler. 'I figger I'll be needin' a rifle and some shells. Got any idea where I can buy any?'

'You'll find Will Telfer's store halfway along the street on your way out of town,' nodded the other. He pursed his lips. 'It's a bit early for him but you might find him open. If not, he'll be over in the saloon.'

'Thanks.' Steve touched spurs to the stallion's flanks, urged the horse out into the street. As he rode along the main street of Anderson, he was aware of the curious glances which followed him. He was used to people staring at him, riding tall and serious-faced in the saddle. He sat the black horse completely relaxed, almost as if he were a part of the animal; and yet to the keen eye there would be seen a strange tension about him, visible only in the set of the mouth and the tight-fisted grip on the reins, an alertness that was instinctive in him.

He sighted the store crowded between two taller wooden buildings and slid from the saddle in front of it, looping the reins casually around the hitching rail.

Will Telfer was a short, stout, balding man and even in the coolness of early morning, there were beads of sweat on his forehead and he continually mopped at his face with a large red handkerchief as though finding the atmosphere unbearably hot.

'Lookin' for a gun, mister?' he asked, leaning his weight on his elbows.

'That's right. A Winchester rifle. Got any new ones in stock?'

'I guess so.' The other turned to the rack on the wall behind him, took down a Winchester and handed it over the counter. Steve examined it carefully, nodded, satisfied. 'I'd also like some shells for it,' he said.

Telfer dug below the counter, came up with a couple of boxes and slid them towards him. 'That'll be thirty dollars the lot,' he said tightly. His glance lifted to Steve's face. 'You intendin' to stay around these parts?'

'Depends,' muttered Steve shortly. 'Reckon I'll be ridin' out when I've finished my business.'

The answer evidently did not satisfy the other and he made as if to say something further, then thought better of it, took the money and folded it carefully.

Thrusting the rifle into the scabbard of the saddle, Steve swung up and moved his mount slowly along the street towards the edge of town. The sun was well up now and the clouds which had gathered close to the eastern horizon at dawn, had dissipated, leaving the sky a cloudless blue from which the sun shone with some semblance of its growing heat.

Outside of town, the trail twisted and wound among tumbled boulders which continued all the way to the bridge spanning the curve of the river. Wooden planks sounded hollowly as he rode over it, then continued down again onto the open rangeland. Half an hour later, he entered timber, the tall pines lifting high around him and he knew he was on the right trail to the Lazy Y ranch.

CHAPTER II

TANGLED TRAILS

Cal Marsden had spent a sleepless night and morning had brought no better edge to his temper. Now, as he stood facing his foreman, the lines around his petulant mouth deepened. 'I should have listened to you, Silvers. Those bungling fools. They take on a stage with only one good shot among the passengers and then two of them have to get themselves killed and the other three ride off without finishing the job. Now that girl has got to Anderson and there ain't any way we can stop her getting through to their place.'

'It might be easy enough to lay an ambush along the trail. It's more'n fifteen miles from town to the Gantry place and there are plenty of spots where an accident could happen.'

No! ' Marsden's tone was sharp. 'We can't afford to do that, not with this marshal in the territory. He'll start puttin' two and two together and comin' up with the right answers. I'll have to go through with this as I originally planned. I'm reckonin' on the marshal comin' here soon. If I can talk him into ridin' out and arrestin' Gantry, it might still be possible to arrange for a lynch mob to take care of him.'

'Could be this marshal ain't the fool you appear to take

him for,' put in the other. 'He may start askin' questions around town before makin' any move.'

'That won't help him none,' muttered Marsden. 'And Blaine will tell the marshal just what I tell him to say.'

'And Gantry? What about him? He may start to do some talkin'.'

Marsden lifted his brows into a tight line. 'As soon as he's safely in jail, I'll take care of Gantry. All I need Enders for is to make it look legal.'

Silvers lifted his head, walked quickly to the window and peered out. 'Reckon you're goin' to get your chance now, boss,' he said quietly. 'This looks like Enders ridin' in now.'

Marsden strode across the room, glanced over the foreman's shoulder, then nodded as he saw the rider coming in along the narrow trail from the pastureland, riding down towards the corral and the courtyard which faced the ranch-house.

He nodded sharply. 'See that those three men stay out of sight until Enders has gone,' he ordered quickly. 'I don't want them meetin' face to face here or it could spell trouble. Big trouble.'

He went out onto the porch and stood there while Steve rode up. Genially, he called out: 'Glad to see you here, Marshal.'

Steve climbed down from the saddle, turned his mount over to the man who came from the side of the house, watched while the stallion was led into the corral, then turned and walked towards Marsden, his spurs raking up little spurts of dust from the courtyard.

He followed the other into the house, seated himself in the chair opposite Marsden and waited for the other to begin. He noticed at once that the rancher seemed ill at ease, a trifle unsure of himself, and wondered why. Then Marsden gave him a bright, sharp glance, took a cigar from his pocket, bit off the end and thrust it between his lips, lighting it with a sulphur match, waving it across the end as he inhaled deeply. He blew smoke into the air, spoke through it.

'You've probably gathered a little of the trouble from my letter, Marshal,' he began. 'I thought it was my duty to tell you of the situation here. Gantry is a wanted man in Kansas and—'

'Just a minute, Marsden,' broke in Steve quickly. 'Where'd you get this information about Gantry? Seems to me you must have done a heap of checkin' to find that out.'

Marsden got to his feet, went over to the large desk in the corner of the room, and took out a notice from one of the drawers. He brought it back to Steve, 'This is the notice I unearthed in Sheriff Blaine's office. I thought I recognised the man. It's Gantry all right.'

Steve stared down at the wanted notice. Ed Colton, wanted for murder and armed robbery.

'And you say that this is Victor Gantry, your neighbour?'

'I know it is. He's changed a little now, but that's him all right. I'll swear out the warrant for his arrest if that's necessary. Reckon I should warn you though, he may decide to resist. I'll be only too glad to send along some of my boys with you when you ride out to his spread.'

'Won't be necessary,' Steve said. The other sounded just a mite too anxious to get Gantry behind bars. There had to be something more behind this than he knew at the moment, and he felt sure that Marsden wasn't after the reward, even though it was five thousand dollars.

Marsden sat bolt upright in his chair. 'But you are goin' to arrest him, aren't you, Marshal? I mean, after all, you're supposed to be the law around these parts and we need protection against men like this. He could start trouble and you know what that would mean.'

'No, I don't know,' said Steve warily. 'What would it mean, Mister Marsden?'

'A full-scale range war, that's what. Don't make any mistake about it, if Gantry makes any trouble, it could get out of hand and nobody could stop it. There are ways here that you evidently don't understand. If you have any pity for the man, keep it for better things. He's a ruthless killer and I want him in jail where he belongs.'

'If he's the killer you say he is, then that's where he'll be,' Steve said slowly.

Marsden did not look too pleased with that answer. He said dryly: 'Hope you ain't doubting my word, Marshal.'

'I like to see every man get an even chance. If he's accused of murder, then I figger he's got the right to defend himself. I'll ride out to his place and question him.'

'Then you're not goin' to arrest him right now?' There was an incredulous note to the other's voice. His lips pressed themselves together into a hard, tight line and a nasty look came into his eyes. 'I got you here, Marshal, to do something that old fool of a sheriff back in Anderson claimed he couldn't. Seems to me that you're just the same as he is, afraid to go up against Gantry. Or it could be that you're thinkin' about that daughter of his who rode in on the stage last night.'

Steve felt the anger mounting in him, but kept it under tight rein. He knew the other was trying to rile him, to get his back up, but he refused to take the bait. 'I'm not arresting a man just on your say-so. Marsden,' he said thinly. 'I'm here to see that the law is carried out. If this man on the poster is Victor Gantry, then he'll be brought in for trial. If he's not, then there's nothin' I can do.'

Marsden's anger was deep in him. His colour burned high in his cheeks and the line of his jaw thrust at Steve; yet he somehow held his feelings down, and his reply was less than Steve had expected. 'Very well, Marshal. Do things your way, but all I ask is that you don't waste any time. We've lived with this man in our midst long enough and if you don't do something pretty soon, I can't be held responsible for what the other citizens of Anderson decide to do. They may even take the law into their own hands and string him up without a trial which is the last thing I would want.'

'I'm sure it is.' Steve got to his feet. 'I'll de everything I can for you, but until I hear the other side of the case, I can't make any arrest.'

Steve saddled, rode out of the courtyard in front of the ranch-house, travelling steadily through the hills, heading west. Through the red-bodied pines which lay heavy all about him, he allowed the horse to take its head, not pushing it, content to ride slowly and turn things over in his mind. There was virtually no underbrush here, only a thick carpet of pine needles that had fallen over many years, muffling the sound of the horse's hoofs so that except for the slight jingle of the metal parts on the bridle, there was no sound, a deep and church-like stillness hanging over the trees. Occasionally, the strong sunlight lanced through an opening in the layer of leaves and branches which interlaced over his head and once, he heard the sharp tap-tapping of a woodpecker on one of the brown, aromatic branches of the pines.

Shortly after noon, he came upon a narrow cattle trail that twisted across the main track through the trees. He paused for a while, staring down at it, noting the fresh imprints of a large bunch of cattle which had recently passed that way. Traffic from one ranchland to the other seemed to be taking place through zig-zag courses in the hills and there might be some truth in Marsden's allegations that some of his cattle were being rustled by Gantry's men. He rode without haste, pausing early in the afternoon, when he judged he was still some distance from the main trail, lit a small fire, cooked bacon and coffee from his roll and then resumed his journey.

It was almost four o'clock, with the sun dipping from its highest point when he came out of the hills and rode down through wide pastureland towards the Gantry ranch. He could just make it out, a cluster of buildings around the ranch itself, barns and bunkhouses coming into view as he rode closer.

He was moving through a narrow ravine that opened up as a wrinkle in the ground when he tensed suddenly in the saddle, sensing the presence of danger close by, but seeing nothing. He would have paid little heed, possibly believing it to be some of Gantry's gunhands herding cattle or riding the perimeter fence, checking for trouble. In a situation like this, with two large spreads lying side by side, tempers and feelings were sure to run high and there were bound to be clashes. Then, abruptly, two horsemen appeared on the lip of the ravine and he felt a slight prick of anxiety as they levelled rifles at him.

'Don't make any false move towards those guns, mister,' said one of them in a harsh, grating tone.

'Doesn't look like one of Marsden's gunhawks,' commented the other. He backed off his mount a little way and slid from the saddle while his companion held his Winchester trained on Steve's chest. There was a heavy moment, threaded with tightness and suspense as the man came forward. He was a short, hatchet-faced individual with the craggy look of a man born out here on the frontier strip. A tough, unbending character, Steve decided inwardly. He would be loyal to one man and shoot anybody on that man's orders.

'Where d'yuh reckon yuh're ridin'?' he asked, thin-lipped. He stood holding the bridle of Steve's mount in a tight fist, the rifle held equally tightly in the other hand, balanced in the crook of his arm.

'I want to have a word with Victor Gantry,' Steve said thinly. 'I didn't expect any welcome like this.'

The other's eyes narrowed. 'What business you got with him?' he asked.

'That's my affair. Now either you stand aside, or you take me to see Gantry. This business of mine is important and I figger he won't like it if he hears you tried to stop me.'

'We've got orders to watch this trail and stop anybody who comes ridin' along it,' said the man still in the saddle. 'Marsden has been tryin' to get a hold on this spread for a long time now and there's no way of tellin' how he'll try the next time.'

'Like you said, I'm not one of Marsden's men. Now, are you goin' to quit talkin' and take me to Gantry?'

For a moment, the men paused, debating that. Then the man in the saddle gave a quick nod. 'All right,' he said tightly. 'Just ride ahead of me. And no tricks mind. I'll have this rifle pointed at your back all the way and I'll pull the trigger the first wrong move you make.'

Steve shrugged, gigged his mount forward and the other fell in behind him. They rode along the trail which widened appreciably as they approached the house. The sound of their mounts in the dry dust of the courtyard brought a man to the door; a tall, broad-shouldered man with dark eyes and unruly hair. He stood looking out over the porch rails as Steve swung down from the saddle. The man who had brought him in dismounted quickly, still holding the rifle on him.

'Found this *hombre* riding the trail just above the peak, boss,' he called, motioning Steve forward. 'Said he was on his way to see you. Claims his business is important, but he wouldn't say what it is.'

'You Victor Gantry?' said Steve quietly, appraising the other. There was certainly a resemblance between the man who stood there, eyeing him curiously, and the picture on that wanted notice which Marsden had shown him; but it was not the close resemblance which Marsden had claimed. He felt a little unsure about the other being the wanted killer.

Gantry gave a slow, lazy nod. 'That's right, mister.' He smiled in a tight, wintry sort of way. 'You say you're lookin' for me?'

'I'd like to talk inside if I may.'

36

For a moment, there was something more than curiosity in the other's face. Then he flicked a quick glance at the man with the rifle, looked back towards Steve. 'All right. Let's go inside.'

In the room that led off the small hallway, the other motioned Steve to a chair, then sank down in one himself, leaning forward, his hands hanging loosely over his thighs. But to Steve's keen gaze it was clear that the other relaxed as though he was under some kind of strain. He patted his shirt front, brought out a cigar and lit it, the sweet-smelling smoke filling the room as he closed his eyes for a moment, then opened them again, fixing his gaze on Steve, keenly and sharply.

'You want a job?' he asked quietly.

Steve shook his head, 'I've already got one,' he said slowly. 'At the moment, it's supposed to be to arrest you on a charge of murder and take you in to stand trial.'

The other jerked upright at that, his face twisting, the look in his eyes hardening. 'You reckon you'll walk out of here alive if you try that?' he said tautly.

Steve gave out a dry answer. 'If I meant to arrest you and any of your men tried to stop me, you'd be dead before they could do anythin'. At the moment I'm trying to get the answers to some questions that have been botherin' me ever since I rode into Anderson. Marsden seems mighty anxious to get you behind bars. He showed me a wanted poster with a face like yours on it, claimed you were wanted in Kansas for murder and armed robbery. He's already tried to get the sheriff in town to arrest you, but he backed down, said it wasn't his affair and he'd have to send for a Federal Marshal.'

Gantry sank back in his chair, some of the tension leaving him. He said softly: 'Why are you telling me all this, Marshal?'

'Let's say that I'm not convinced of your guilt. Seems to me that Marsden had got something back of his mind that

I don't know about and I'd like to know a little more before I start arrestin' anybody.'

'Listen, Marshal,' said the other seriously. 'I don't know anythin' about any killing in Kansas. Whoever that was on the poster you saw, it certainly wasn't me. But I reckon I know why Marsden has done this. He wants my ranch. He's tried to frame me on a charge of rustling and when he couldn't make that stick, he's tried this.'

'It could be that you're right,' conceded Steve.

'Hell, I know I'm right,' said the other tightly. 'He owns nearly all of Anderson. He's got the saloons and the hotel, he owns half of the bank and most of the stores there. Sheriff Blaine is in cahoots with him, does exactly as Marsden says, otherwise he'll lose his job and another man will be elected sheriff in his place.'

'Can you prove any of that?' asked Steve bluntly.

'No, but Blaine may talk if you push him hard enough.'

'That may be somethin' worth lookin' into.'

'Whatever you do, don't underestimate Marsden. He's a big man in this territory and he'll do anythin' to take what he wants. He didn't get to where he is now without trampling over a host of smaller men, buying their land for less than a quarter of its value and if they refused to sell out, he sent in his men to fire their barns and ranch-houses, rustle their cattle, until they were forced to pull out.'

Steve nodded. It was the same old story so common in this part of the country; ruthless men, determined to grab themselves as big a slice of the territory as they could, and not worrying overmuch how they did it, by legal means or otherwise. *Some did not even stop short at murder.*

He made to say something more, but at that moment the door opened and he glanced round swiftly to see the girl standing there. She was staring at him across the room and the look in her eyes told him that she had discovered who he was and why he was there.

Gantry got to his feet, took a step forward and said:

'Beth, I want you to meet Steve Enders. He's—'

'I know exactly who he is, Father,' said the girl and there was a trace of bitter anger in her voice. 'Maybe you don't know why he's here. He came because Cal Marsden sent for him to arrest you on a trumped-up charge of murder. I heard about it in Anderson just before I left this morning. And I thought you might be impartial when you were on that stage, fighting off Marsden's gunmen.'

'Now see here, Miss Gantry,' began Steve. 'I've already had a talk with your father and—'

'And he's explained the position to me quite satisfactorily, Beth,' said Gantry firmly. 'He's quite ready to listen to everything with an open mind. He doesn't intend to arrest me just because Marsden says so. I reckon we can straighten this thing out between us.'

The girl simmered down at that, but her glance was still hostile, still suspicious. She stepped back and Steve saw her self-assurance return as she faced him. 'I didn't think you would be so willing to take our word against Marsden's,' she said slowly.

'When you have a job like mine that brings you into contact with all sorts of people, you learn not to go by first impressions. It usually happens that when somebody like Marsden asks for a man to be arrested, there's a little more to it than a simple case of a citizen trying to help the law. I'm wondering what's at the back of Marsden's request. Until I find out, I'll scout around and pick up what information I can. Then, if it proves necessary, I'll make an arrest.'

'Be careful you don't find yourself in trouble. Marsden won't hold his hand just because you're a Federal marshal.' She watched him as she gave the warning and when he merely nodded and smiled, her expression grew lighter, less tense and suspicious, until she was smiling too. 'You evidently don't know this country, Marshal,' she went on softly. 'There are men here with habits like prairie-wolves.

Marsden is one of them, believe me.'

'You said when you came in that it was some of Marsden's men who tried to hold up the stage. Any idea who they were and why they did it?'

'They had to be Marsden's men,' she declared hotly. 'There's no one else who would do it. Seems to me that if Marsden wants my father out of the way so that he can move in and take over the ranch, he'll need to get me out of the way too, because he won't succeed as long as I'm alive. Those men weren't after gold. They wanted to kill me.'

Steve's eyes grew very still as he turned that thought over in his mind. It seemed one answer at least, as to why that particular stage had been attacked and not that leaving Chester two days later with the payroll which would have seemed to have been the logical one to stop.

'Could be that the driver recognised some of them,' he said after a brief pause. 'None of them seemed to be wearing masks when they attacked us. That's a curious thing for a start.'

The girl continued to watch him; she was puzzled and she was also uncertain and this expression gave a softness to her features.

Victor Gantry said: 'Ain't no point in ridin' back into town tonight, Marshal. We can put you up here and you can leave in the morning.'

Steve nodded his thanks. 'I'll leave just after breakfast,' he said.

Even so soon after supper, the main street of Anderson was filled with celebrants coming out of the saloons where Marsden had given free drinks all round. No one had paused to ask why he was being so generous with his money, but Sheriff Blaine felt a trifle uneasy as he watched the men on the street. There was something brewing. He could feel it in his bones. Trouble always seemed to bring him an advance warning in this way, almost as though he had some kind of sixth sense that responded to it. At the corner of the street where the bank jutted out, a large group of the men swung round to the end saloon, thrust open the doors and went inside, the doors swinging shut behind them.

Blaine sat at his desk with two of the lamps lit, throwing long shadows into the corners of the room. He had left the celebrations early and come back to his office. It looked as if Marsden might be getting these men into a fighting mood, ready to lead them out against Gantry. But if he did that, he would run into Enders, the marshal. By now, Blaine was certain that the marshal had left Marsden's place and ridden on to see Gantry and check these accusations out with him. If he got past the men Gantry had watching the trails of his spread without being shot on sight, he might even now be talking things over with the other, getting at the truth. Blaine was reasonably sure in his own mind that the poster Marsden had taken from him some time before, was not that of Gantry, even though there was, admittedly, a slight resemblance.

He heard horses converging in front of his office and glanced through the dust-covered window into the growing dusk. Marsden's horsemen and the rancher himself were lined up in front of the building at the hitching rail.

Marsden came in a couple of minutes later, threw a quick glance around the office, then seated himself unasked in the chair in front of the desk. He said tightly: 'I suppose you've heard that this marshal has ridden on over to Gantry's place.'

'You mean he's going to arrest him on your say-so?' Blaine sounded surprised.

'No, damnit, he ain't,' thundered the other. 'He's gone to talk things over with him. Now that could mean trouble for me, big trouble.'

'So what do you reckon I can do about it?' asked Blaine.

Marsden half rose to his feet, knuckles standing out under the flesh of his fingers. Then he sank back again, forced himself to relax. 'He'll probably come ridin' into town tomorrow, asking more questions. I aim to see that he doesn't stay around long enough to get any of the answers.'

Blaine's eyes narrowed to mere slits. He shook his head. 'I think you're makin' a big mistake, Marsden. If you're reckoning on killin' him, I'd better warn you he's one of the fastest shots in the territory. Make one little mistake and you're dead.'

Marsden smiled thinly. 'There are more ways of killin' a man than facing him with a gun in your hand. That's a fool's way when you're dealing with a man like Steve Enders and I know it.'

'That why you're getting everybody steamed up with whiskey?'

Marsden twisted his lips tautly. 'They won't give you any trouble if that's what's worryin' you,' he said harshly. 'I reckoned that if I could get Enders here everythin' would be taken care of. I see I was wrong. Once he starts diggin' around, he may find out things I want to keep hidden.' He got to his feet, stood looking down at the lawman with an expression of utter contempt on his face. 'And as for you, Blaine, if you've got any ideas of tryin' to give him any information behind my back, I'd forget 'em. You're in this as deep as I am and I know enough about you to hang you twice over. Think on that before you do anythin' stupid.'

Blaine seemed to cringe visibly in front of the other's gaze. After Marsden had left, riding along the street in the direction of the saloon, his men trailing after him, Blaine sat at his desk for a long moment, staring into the flickering yellow light of the oil lamps. He was a failure, he thought to himself; a coward, not fitted for the position he held. Yet he knew that he could not go against Marsden. The other had him in a cleft stick, could do exactly as he had threatened.

Why in God's name had Marsden brought that marshal here in the first place? If they had worked things differently, it ought to have been possible to get rid of Gantry without

42

all of this fuss. He was against violence himself, but Marsden had run several of the smaller ranchers out of the territory without too much trouble in the old days; he felt sure they could do the same with Gantry. True the other was a bigger and more powerful man than any of these men had been, but Marsden had enough men to force a showdown and he felt certain that the girl would not stay if trouble did break out.

Lighting a cigarette over one of the lamps, he leaned back and tried to stop the shaking in his limbs, drawing the smoke into his lungs. A strange sickness was in his mind and he tried to swallow the feeling, to bring back a little of his self-pride. There was one thing sure. Enders would be riding into danger when he came into Anderson the next day as he was sure to do.

CHAPTER III

BUSHWHACKER!

Steve left the Gantry ranch around eight o'clock. Even at that time, the sun was well up, shining with a warmth that struck through his jacket. He rode out of the wide court-yard, over the brow of the hill and then downgrade, now on the trail and now in deep timber with only a pale green light filtering through the canopy of leaves overhead, and the sharp aromatic smell of the pine needles in his nostrils, with the heat trapped in the ground, just beginning to rise and dispel the coolness. He deliberately clung to the narrow trail that kept inside the timber for as far as possible. The girl had warned him of trouble before he had left, while they had been seated at breakfast and although he felt an urgent restlessness in him, he kept any recklessness from his mind. Marsden might decide to take the law into his own hands. He had fallen in with Steve's decision to visit Gantry and try to get his side of the story a little too readily for it to have been convincing. There was the feeling at the back of his mind that perhaps the other was already putting some of his own plans into action and the uneasiness increased a little in Steve's mind as he rode through the tall pines. He threw off a couple of creeks before noon and by this time the heat was really intense, a beating pressure that lay on the land like the flat of some heavy, mighty hand.

At this rate, he would be in town some time in late afternoon. He had already decided to have a word with the grizzled old driver of the stage. He had told them he had been driving that stage for close on forty years and even allowing for the fact that he might have been exaggerating a little, he still ought to know most of the faces in these parts and if he had managed to catch a glimpse of any of those bandits, he should have known them.

He recalled the face of the man he had seen on that horse which had leapt from the ledge of the canyon, almost in the path of the stage. There should be no difficulty in recognising that man again if he saw him. He'd tried to keep his eyes open while he had been at Marsden's place, but he'd seen nobody resembling him.

Leaving the timber, he reached the main trail and stayed with it all the way into Anderson. The town seemed quiet as ever as he rode into the main street; too quiet, he reflected, eyes wary. He had the unshakable feeling of trouble ready to break. Acting on impulse, he reined his mount at the end of the street, cast about him for any sign of trouble, but he could see nothing. There were half a dozen horses tethered in front of one of the saloons, and further on, a group of men drifted into the hotel, ready for the evening meal. The wind flowing down from the hills and soughing along the street held a coolness in it that was like a balm to his heated features. With an effort, he tried to shake the feeling of uneasiness from him, but it refused to go.

Gently, he eased the Colts in their holsters, urged his mount forward and walked it along the street, his eyes drifting from right to left. This was a feeling he had experienced on several occasion in the past and he had learned from bitter experience never to doubt it, never to ignore it. The little spot between his shoulder blades began to itch but he deliberately refrained from looking round. Not until he rode past one of the saloons and noticed that here, in

45

contrast to the rest of the street, there were no men lounging in the wicker chairs on the boardwalk, did he realise
that it was here that the danger lay.

The shot whiplashed at the very instant that Steve caught
a glimpse of the sudden movement to his right in the
mouth of the small dark alley that ran back from the main
street probably to link up with one of the smaller streets to
the rear of the town. The bullet skimmed Steve's shoulder
as he dropped from his mount, hitting the ground hard, but
putting the horse between himself and his unknown
assailant. His guns leapt from their holsters even as he
struck the street and rolled over, body slewing round as he
twisted to face the alley. Through his horse's legs, he
glimpsed the dark shadow that moved to the other side of
the alley mouth in an obvious attempt to get a better shot at
him. Clearly the marksman did not know for sure whether
he had been hit or not, and if he had, whether the shot had
been fatal. Steve's raking eyes took in everything in a single
glance and a split second after he hit the ground, the guns
in his hands spoke, sending lead into the alley. His first
shots whined shrilly off the walls of the buildings, screaming
off the brick in wild ricochet, but his next shot found target
in flesh and he heard a man curse, give a loud yell and saw
the flgure rolling back into the alley before getting to its
feet and begin to run back in an odd, crab-like scuttling.

Thrusting himself to his feet, running in front of his
mount, Steve made the mouth of the alley, pushed himself
hard against the wall of the nearby building and peered
cautiously round it. Vaguely, he was able to make out the
scraping of the bushwhacker's boots as he tried to get away.
His man wasn't fatally hit, he knew for certain, but by hell,
if this dry-gulcher wanted to nail him, he'd have to get him
in his sights first to get an accurate shot at him.

Steve did not stop at the corner of the alley for more
than five seconds. Swiftly, duckling low, he ran into it, saw
the narrow boardwalk that ran along one side, with a

wooden overhang which afforded plenty of dark shadow, and ran along it, sure that the hammer of his booted heels on the wooden boardwalk gave away his position. Digging in with toes and heels, he sprinted to the far end of the alley, saw as he had suspected, that it linked with a wider street that ran at right angles across it. The street was filled with wooden boxes, piles of rubbish, behind which a man could hide and draw a bead on him from cover.

There was no sign of the dry-gulcher, no sound of retreating footsteps and Steve knew that the other was still there, crouched down out of sight behind one of these piles of rubbish. Cautiously, he edged forward, the guns hefted in his hands, his fingers tight on the triggers. He waited, felt the familiar hatred for a dry-gulcher pour through him as he stood there, chilling him and he knew that he would not have to wait long before the other gave himself away. It was this taut waiting and the fact that he had been wounded that would eventually break the other down. Behind him, he heard a confused shouting from the direction of the main street. Sheriff Blaine would come running pretty soon to see what the trouble was, he thought inwardly, although if this was more of Marsden's doing, the sheriff would wait until one of the men was dead before moving in.

Suddenly, he heard a low, groaning sigh come out of the man. It was the sudden need for air and the inability to hold in the pain which made the other betray himself. He seemed to know it too, for he suddenly began firing recklessly along the street, bullets hammering off the walls and boxes in murderous ricochet.

Keeping his head down, crouching a little, Steve called out: 'I'm coming forward,' and edged a little to one side. He meant to make his man back away from where he was hiding. The shots had already placed the other on the far side of the street. He made out the scrape of the other's body and when he heard it he drew up his guns and laid them on the open patch of ground behind the boxes where the other was crouched, waiting patiently for the man's nerve to break. But the other did not back away. Instead, he seemed to realise what Steve's plan was for he suddenly managed to lunge to his feet and run forward, his head low, pausing as he reached the point where the street and alley met, slewing wildly, bringing up his gun in a quick movement.

Steve dug in his boots, rested his back and shoulders against the wall and squeezed both triggers, working them swiftly, ripping out a sharp tattoo of deadly shots.

The man reared to his toes, hung there for a brief moment, then reeled back as the lead slammed into him, arching his body. His gun exploded, but he was already falling as the last ounce of strength in him brought the pressure to bear on the trigger and the shot went high into the air over Steve's head. Then the other's body crashed down onto one of the wooden boxes, smashing it to splinters with his weight, rolling sideways with a threshing of arms and legs.

Twisting the guns, Steve moved forward, ready to pump more shots into the other's body if he was shamming death. But there was no movement and the other flopped back limply as Steve turned him over with the toe of his boot, found himself staring down into the black-bearded face of the man he had seen on that horse, leaping down from the lip of the ravine on to the mountain trail when the stage had been held up. There would be no more trouble from him, he thought savagely, but there would also be no information as to who had hired him to try to kill him.

Dead men told no tales, and it was certain that Marsden, if he was at the back of this, would not talk.

Straightening, he turned as there came the clatter of footsteps running along the alley. Sheriff Blaine burst into view, his gun drawn as he came forward slowly, picking his way carefully towards Steve over the piled up rubbish. If there was any disappointment in him that it was Steve who was still alive and not the other man, none of it showed on his face as he went forward and stared down at the killer's face. Then he thrust his Colt back into leather and looked up at Steve.

'You know this man, Enders?' he said softly.

'Not by name,' Steve said. 'But I recognise him. He's one of the men who attacked the stage.'

'You sure of that?'

Steve nodded emphatically. 'I'd recognize that face anywhere. He was the leader of that outlaw gang.'

'Any idea why he'd take a shot at you?' The other's gaze searched his face. 'He did shoot at you, didn't he? I heard the firin' but didn't see anythin' of it.'

'He tried to bushwhack me as I rode into town. Offhand, I'd say he was hired to kill me.'

'Got any idea who might have hired him?' There was a bright, speculative look in the sheriff's eyes, a tightening of his lips.

'Could have been either Marsden or Gantry,' he said easily. 'I reckon they're the only people with an axe to grind as far as I'm concerned.'

'Don't make sense that Marsden would want you killed,' grunted Blaine. 'He asked you to come here, didn't he?'

'That's right, only he may think that because I haven't arrested Gantry already, that I'm not doing things fast enough for him and he's decided to take matters into his own hands and push things on a little. And he'd have to get me out of the way to do that.'

The best part of a minute passed before Steve said, tautly: 'I gather that you don't recognise this man.'

Blaine shook his head. 'Never seen him before in my life,' he muttered. He looked around at the men gathered round in a small group. 'Any of you men seen this *hombre* before around town?'

The men shook their heads. One said: 'He ain't one of Marsden's regular hired hands anyway, that's for sure.'

'Then you got no idea at all why he should try to bush-whack you, Marshal?' asked Blaine again.

'Not at the moment. I figger he's workin' for somebody in this town. Just another saddle-bum by the look of him, ready and willin' to sell his gun to the highest bidder. I reckon he's paid a high enough price for that privilege.' He turned, strode away from the group of men gathered around the dead gunhawk.

Blaine came hurrying after him. He said urgently: 'I don't want you to take this wrong, Marshal, but I want no trouble in this town. And if you start anything with Marsden that you can't finish, this place is likely to bust wide open.'

Steve swung on him, his face suffused with a sudden anger as he took the meaning behind the other's words. 'Just what are you tryin' to say, Blaine? That I ought to forget this little incident, that I should ride on out of town just because I ain't doin' things the way Cal Marsden wants 'em done? Seems to me there's somethin' far wrong goin' on around these parts and I aim to find out what it is. First Marsden wants Gantry thrown into jail on a trumped-up charge of murder and robbery. I've talked with Gantry and I'm ready to stake my reputation that he's not the man shown in that poster which Marsden carries around with him. Where he got that idea from I don't know. But he sure wants Gantry in jail.'

Blaine's eyes flicked away. He looked a trifle uneasy. Then he drew himself up tautly, tried to get back a little of his lost dignity. 'You've got your job to do, Marshal,' he muttered stiffly, 'and I have mine. Here in Anderson, I represent the law and your say-so goes for very little, if anythin'. If you're sure that Gantry ain't this wanted killer, then your job is finished. I reckon that for the good of the town, you ought to ride on.'

Steve smiled thinly. 'You don't get rid of me as easily as that, Sheriff,' he grated. 'I figger I'll stick around a little longer. I've got the feeling that if I do, sooner or later, the *hombre* who's at the back of all this, will be forced out into the open and I'll be waitin' when he is. In the meantime, I'm goin' to have a little talk with that stage-driver.'

Blaine took a hesitant step forward as if he intended to stop the other, then evidently thought better of it, for he moved away. Shrugging, he gave Steve an enigmatic glance and turned away, walking across the street and into the saloon.

As he strode along the boardwalk, feeling the coolness of the evening air blow about him, Steve turned over what had happened in his mind, trying to find some logical explanation of it all. Somebody clearly wanted him out of the way, that was for sure. He didn't think it was Gantry, although if he was wrong about the other, and Victor Gantry did have another name down in Kansas, he might do all that he could to get rid of him before he could cause trouble, if only to protect himself and his daughter. There were plenty of men who had been killers in their young days, who were trying to settle down in out-of-the-way places like this, where they hoped to live out the rest of their lives, some with their ill-gotten gains, unnoticed and forgotten. On the other hand, Marsden was an equally likely candidate. It was abundantly clear that he too, had something to hide. He obviously had a big hold on this town and when a man like Marsden gave orders, little men such as Sheriff Blaine didn't try to talk back or question those orders, they merely carried them out. Marsden also wanted to get his hands on Gantry's spread. But if the stage-driver had recognised any of those bandits who had tried to hold up the stage, it might provide him with a lead, a clue on which to base something.

Inside the stage office, he found a harassed-looking clerk seated behind a small desk, his coat off, shirt sleeves rolled up above the elbows.

'If you've come here looking for a seat on the stage tomorrow, you're out of luck, Mister,' said the other in a whining, nasal voice. 'Since Clem was shot up on the stage a couple of days ago, we only got one driver and he can only take them out every two days working non-stop.'

'I know. It's Clem I want to see. I reckon he might be able to identify some of those men who held up the stage.' The other regarded him with a spark of curiosity in his deep-set eyes. 'Well now, I don't know—'

Steve held out the silver badge, saw the instant change in the other's expression. 'Oh, sure, that's different, Marshal. He's through there.' The clerk moved his head at the open door of a room at the end of the short passage leading off from the office.

It was a bedroom, obviously where the drivers slept whenever they came in at the end of a run. Here, Steve found the old driver propped up on pillows, naked from the waist up, a broad white bandage looped around his shoulder and one arm. He glanced up at Steve from under thick, bushy, grey brows drawn into a straight line. He said hoarsely: 'If you've just come to—' He broke off, stared more intently, trying to lean forward a little, gasping as a fresh stab of pain went through him. 'Say, ain't you the *hombre* who fought off them critters and brought the stage in?'

'That's right, old-timer,' nodded Steve. He sat down on the woven chair by the bed. 'You feel up to talkin'?'

'Sure. Reckon I could drive that stage only the danged sawbones says I'm too old now to be able to get onto my feet so soon after havin' a bit of lead taken out of my shoulder. Hell, in the old days, when there was Indians roaming those trails we used to drive the stages with more'n this inside us and think nothin' of it. I mind one time when we were—'

'All right, I believe you,' interrupted Steve, holding up his hand to break off the other's flow of words. 'But I need your help.'

'You lookin' for them polecats?' muttered the other weakly. He lay back on the pillows as if his recent outburst had weakened him.

52

'I found one. He tried to bushwhack me this evening when I rode into town.'

Clem drew his brows even more tightly together. 'So it was you they were after. I figgered it had be somethin' like that. Weren't no gold on that stage.'

'I'm not so sure whether they were tryin' to get me that time – or whether they were after the girl.'

'Vic Gantry's daughter?'

'You know her then?'

'Knew her when she was only knee-high to a grasshopper,' affirmed the other, forcing a quick, strained grin. 'Didn't recognise her on the stage though, she's growed some since I last saw her. But I did hear somebody mention her name back in Chester before we pulled out. Figgered it had to be her.'

Steve nodded. 'The gunhawk who tried to kill me was the leader of those outlaws. Tall, big-boned, black-bearded. I was hopin' you might have seen him when they hit the stage.'

'Sure, I saw 'em all, clear as I'm seein' you,' declared the other positively as he shifted himself into a more comfortable position on the bed, 'Funny thing though, weren't one of 'em wearin' a mask. Not one.'

'Did you recognise any of 'em? Could they have been some of Marsden's men?'

The other's brow furrowed in deep concentration, then he shook his head slowly, frowning a little as a spasm of pain lanced through his body. 'Never saw any of 'em before in my life. They sure weren't Marsden's hired hands.'

Steve let his breath go in little pinches through his nostrils and sank back on the chair. He realised that he had been wishing for too much. It wasn't going to be easy to pin this on Marsden.

'He's goin' to make big trouble, Marsden.' Sheriff Blaine ran his tongue over dry lips. 'I said it was a mistake to bring a marshal in to do your dirty work for you, particularly a man like Enders. Now we've got to—'

'Shut up, will you!' roared Marsden harshly. 'I've got to think this out.' He went over to the window and stared out across the corral of the ranch.

'One thing, he won't be able to tie up that hold-up or the shootin' with me. None of those men are known in these parts. Just a bunch of sidewinders I found camping on my land.'

'That may be so,' argued Blaine. 'But if this marshal goes around town and starts askin' questions, particularly about any title deeds to those ranches you took over, and how they were notarised, we're in trouble.'

'I'll take care of that if it ever happens,' snapped Marsden. His big hands clenched and unclenched behind his back as he tried to keep control of his feelings. 'But in the meantime we've got to fix Enders.'

'Like I said, that ain't goin' to be easy. You saw what happened to that gunman who reckoned he could shoot him down from ambush. He figgered that was the easy way of doin' it, cut him down before he knew what was happenin'. But it didn't turn out that way. The marshal is like a striking rattler and he seems to know just when there's trouble lyin' in wait for him.'

'Then maybe it's time we used a little cunning and baited a trap for him that he can't wriggle out of.'

'You got an idea how to do that?'

'I reckon so. I'll have to think it out a little more and I'll need your help to fix it.' He swung to face the sheriff, felt a momentary anger at the way the other had that scared look in his eyes. 'And I'm sure you're goin' to help me, Blaine, because if you don't—' He deliberately left the remainder of the threat unsaid.

'OK I'll help,' blustered the other. He pushed himself to his feet. 'But it had better not fail this time. I wouldn't want to try on a straight-away draw with this marshal.' There was a half grin on his thin lips.

Steve Enders walked along the boardwalk, seeing the town come alive after the heat of the noon sun. The saloon directly ahead of him was full of noise, with a tinny piano hammering out one of the songs of the deep South which had been taken over by the North during the Civil War. Pushing open the batwing doors, he strode in. The town had been remarkably quiet after the shooting and he was beginning to think that it had perhaps settled down a little. Maybe whoever had been behind that bushwhacking had thought twice about the matter and decided there was no point in pushing his luck too far.

At a corner card table, four men were playing poker, their heads bowed over their cards, only the rattle of coins breaking the silence from that direction. Other men were ranged along the bar and Steve thought he recognised one of the men standing there. The face seemed familiar, but at the moment he couldn't place it and the thought intrigued and worried him. He liked to know exactly where he stood in a place like this. Beside the man was a big, raw-boned man, his skin burned to the colour of old chap leather from the sun along the southern borders, the flesh tight over his face, lips drawn together in a cruel expression.

The chunky bartender moved across to Steve, stood with his hands flat on top of the bar, eyeing him inquiringly.

'Whiskey,' said Steve quietly. He took the bottle which the other placed in front of him, poured a glassful and motioned to the other to leave the half-filled bottle where it was. The bartender nodded, moved away as one of the men further along the bar called out to him.

There were perhaps two dozen men standing at the bar. Some of them had turned to watch Steve appraisingly as he had walked in. A tall, well-dressed man, standing a few yards away, turned and said something to the big, raw-boned man and they both laughed loudly. Steve felt a little of the tight anger beginning to rise in him, guessed that the remark which had been passed had concerned him.

There was the low buzz of conversation. Then it stopped as a woman came out onto the small stage at the far end of the bar-room. The pianist, his hat pulled well over his eyes, gave a rolling flourish of notes on the piano. Steve turned and glanced at the woman as she swept forward until she stood in the middle of the stage, her glance sweeping coldly over the assembled men, pausing at none until her gaze rested momentarily on Steve. For an instant, her eyes paused as she looked at him. An instant, no longer, then they drifted away again, around the room, taking in every-one there. As she sang, all noise in the saloon stopped and even the tall man seemed to have relaxed a little, so that his mouth was no longer set in such a cruel streak.

When the song was finished, there was an outburst of applause, loud calls for her to sing again, but she shook her head and left the stage.

Steve glanced round, caught the bartender's eye and motioned him forward. 'Who's that big *hombre* yonder?' he asked softly.

The bartender's eyes flicked sideways, then he looked back. 'That's Slim Silvers, Cal Marsden's foreman,' he said in a low whisper. A new look came to his face. 'Now see here, mister,' he began, keeping his voice low. 'I don't want any trouble in here.'

'I don't know that there'll be any,' Steve muttered. 'I just wanted to know who he is. Seems to me I've seen that other fella standing beside him somewhere before.'

The bartender pursed his lips. 'He came in here for the first time a couple of days ago. I ain't seen him around before then. Looks like some saddle tramp that Marsden's signed up onto his payroll.'

'Could be,' said Steve in a non-committal tone. 'And the well-dressed man?'

The other gave him a quick, sharp look. 'Seems to me

you're askin' a heap of questions,' he said dryly.

'Mebbe so. But I'd be obliged if you'd answer 'em.'

The bartender blinked, bit back the sharp retort which was clearly on the tip of his tongue. 'That's Will Carew, the banker. A mighty important citizen in town.'

Steve sipped his drink and when he said nothing further, the bartender drifted away, mopping at the top of the bar with his rag, occasionally glancing back in Steve's direction, his face puzzled.

Carew said loudly: 'If you ask me, Silvers, he won't last another day in town. That was a lucky shot he got in. Won't happen the next time.'

The big foreman laughed, a deep rumble in his throat. He banged his empty glass on the bar and the bartender moved forward quickly to refill it. 'Whoever that *hombre* was, he couldn't shoot straight, that's for sure.'

Steve poured himself another drink. Through the glass at the back of the bar, he noticed that everyone in the saloon with the exception of the four poker players were watching the proceedings at the bar with ill-disguised interest, aware that something was about to break, that there may be gunplay soon. He gave no indication that he had heard what the others had said, keeping a tight rein on his temper, guessing that this conversation was being carried on loudly for the express purpose of riling him.

'I did hear,' Carew was saying, his voice slightly drunk, 'that he went to pay a courtesy call on Gantry, that killer from Kansas way who's been living like a lord in these parts for nearly as long as I can remember. Wonder what a man who's supposed to be upholding the law was doing with that snake.'

'Could be he's in cahoots with him,' roared Silvers. 'Seems to me I've heard of crooked lawmen before, hiding behind their badges.'

Steve tightened his grip on the glass in his hand, gulped down the whiskey in a single swallow, felt it burn his throat and down into his stomach in an expanding haze of warmth. He knew that the bartender was watching him closely, trying to assess what he meant to do.

Carew swung round and stared directly at Steve for the first time. Then he pushed himself away from the bar and came over to Steve, staggering a little, clearly the worse for drink. Steve felt the tightness grow in him, but continued to stare in front of him, across the bar.

'We're talking about you, Marshal.' Carew stood before him, peering at him closely as if short-sighted. 'I say you're a disgrace to that badge you carry, throwing in your lot with a killer like Gantry.'

Steve turned slowly, letting his glance rest on the other. 'You're drunk, Mister Carew,' he said slowly, clearly, 'otherwise I don't think you'd be sayin' such things. Either that, or you've been put up to it by those men you're drinkin' with.'

'Now, see here,' roared Silvers. 'I don't take that from any man, marshal or no – and it don't matter to me how fast they say you are with a gun.'

Carew held up his hand, to silence the other. He went on loudly, eyes trying to focus on Steve. 'You ain't denying that you went to see Gantry.'

'No, I ain't denying it. I went to have a talk with him about these accusations that are bein' spread around by Cal Marsden.'

Carew's brows went up at that. He grinned foolishly. 'You know damned well, Marshal, that he's a low-down killer. And he's been living among us like a respected citizen for more'n thirty years. Reckon if you won't lock him up for trial, we'll have to get a citizens' committee together and do something about it ourselves.'

'You've drunk too much,' said Steve. He turned his head away. What happened next was almost too quick for the eye to take in. Carew, stung by that last remark, fumbled for the gun under his frock coat. Before his hand could drop to it, Steve had whirled and the flat of his hand caught the banker across the elbow, knocking his arm sideways and in the same movement, his fist caught the other in the chest, hurling him backward, completely off balance. The other crashed against one of the tables, overturned it, and lay still as his head cracked against the stone floor with a sickening crunch.

As he glanced up, whirling to face Silvers, Steve noticed that the man who had been standing next to the big foreman had gone, had slipped out of the saloon during the few moments that his eyes had left the other.

Silvers was already going for his guns, hands dropping like striking snakes, his shoulders contracted. He was fast and he thought he had the drop on Steve, but he relaxed and backed up instantly, a surprised expression on his hard face as the guns in Steve's hands were levelled on his chest while his own were only half drawn from their holsters.

'I ought to kill you, Silvers,' Steve said thickly. 'I figger you picked this argument just to try to get the drop on me.'

'If that's the way you kill your men, go ahead,' grunted the other hoarsely. He gave Steve a quick look that was so sharp it might have cut his throat.

Out of the corner of his eye, Steve caught a glimpse of the man behind the bar moving nervously, his hands now out of sight. He said slowly: 'Get those hands of yours where I can see 'em, bartender, or I'll blow your head off.'

Hastily, the other lifted his hands back on top of the bar, lips twisting into a grimace of fear, eyes wide in his head.

'That's better.' Steve locked back to Silvers. 'Unshuck that gun belt,' he ordered tightly.

The other hesitated. 'You figgerin' on shootin' me down in cold blood?' he said sneeringly. His tone was not quite as sure of itself as he tried to sound.

'Drop that gunbelt.' Steve moved the Colts menacingly and the other lowered his hands, unfastened the heavy metal buckle and let the belt fall to the floor.

'You seemed to be pretty big as far as words are

59

concerned,' Steve said, thrusting the guns back into leather. 'Let's see if you can back 'em up.'

'Why you pipsqueak,' roared the foreman, 'I'll kill you with my bare hands and—'

His warning had been merely a feint for what he intended to do. He never finished the sentence, but came in with his arms and huge, bunched fists flailing savagely, hoping to pulverise the man in front of him. Steve ducked the other's wild swings easily, judged the man's speed and distance and moved in, stepping slightly to one side. His right fist travelled less than six inches but it had all of his wiry weight behind it and the other flew backward from the blow, arms wide, legs buckling under him. He crashed into a table close beside the unconscious figure of the banker, knocked it over on its side, flailing out sideways as he went down, trying desperately to clutch at something that would break his fall.

Steve waited, eyes casting about him, ready for any wrong move from the others watching, but they all seemed to believe that Silvers would win this apparently uneven battle, in spite of this first setback. Silvers struggled to get to his feet, lips twisted into a snarling grimace of animal hatred. His eyes were narrowed to mere slits and he made a roaring, almost bleating sound as he lunged forward, not getting to his feet as Steve had expected him to, but throwing himself almost horizontally along the ground, catching Steve around the legs. Unable to maintain his balance, Steve went over backwards, lashing out with all the strength in his legs in an attempt to loosen the other's tight grip. But Silvers hung on grimly, teeth clenched, hands locked as his arms encircled Steve's legs, holding him down.

A savage right, as the other suddenly released his hold, struck Steve at the side of the head, making his teeth chatter. The lamps in the saloon dimmed momentarily and there was a dull roaring at the back of his temples that drowned out every other sound. Silvers loomed over him, his mouth open, drooling a little as he swung back with his arm for another blow. Swiftly, Steve jerked his head to one side and the foreman yelped in sudden agony as his knuckled fists struck the floor where the marshal's head had been a split second earlier. Before he could recover from his surprise, Steve pulled back his legs, got them under the other's body and thrust up with all of his might. Silver yelled loudly, went flying backwards, crashing against the front of the bar, all of the air in his lungs whooshing out in a bleating gasp under the shattering impact. He hung there for a moment, dazed by the bone-shaking blow.

Steve got to his feet, stood there for a moment, scarcely able to move, knowing that he had the other at his mercy, but trying desperately to focus his eyes which seemed blurred by tears. Then, without warning, something caught him a savage blow at the side of the head and everything danced in front of his vision. He half dropped to his knees, caught a fragmentary glimpse of the man at his back, with the gun held in his fingers, a gun that had been reversed, ready to strike him again. Without pausing to think, he kicked out with one booted foot, caught the other on the ankle. The man howled in agony, fell back, the gun dropping from his fingers.

Steve braced himself, aware that Silvers was already on his feet, coming towards him again, his face murderous, his eyes filled with the glint of killing fever. The other was not going to stop now until he had killed his opponent. With a wild rush, the big foreman came in, kicked out with one foot. The blow would have killed Steve instantly had it landed, it had all of the other's weight behind it, and it was aimed at the side of his head. But he had moved in that second before Silvers swung and the toe of the other's boot merely glanced along his shoulder, but such was the tremendous power behind it, that the blow numbed him completely, sent a stab of pain lancing along his arm, all the way to his fingertips. He moved the other way, sidestepping,

61

so that the foreman swung past him, fighting desperately to maintain his balance. He blundered into one of the circular tables, caught at the edge with both hands and hung there for a moment, pulling air down into his lungs before turning.

Steve took the opportunity to shake his head in an attempt to clear it of the woolly fuzziness, forcing air into his body. His chest hurt as if every rib had been cracked or bruised and each breath he took stung like fire. But it cleared his head and he was ready and waiting by the time Silvers had turned and was moving in for the kill, arms hanging loosely by his sides, obviously hoping to wrap them around Steve's body and crush the life out of him in a bear hug.

Backing off before the other could get to him, Steve leaned a little to one side to let Silvers spend the full fury of his blind attack. Getting in close, he sent a hard right to the other's face, felt the man's nose give under the punch, saw blood spurt down his chin from the force of the blow, then immediately rattled in two short blows to the other's stomach. Silvers uttered a shrill retching sound through wide-open lips. His hands went down to grab at his stomach and Steve threw in a swinging uppercut just as the other bent. It caught the big foreman full on the chin, sent his head back on his shoulders, lifting his whole body as if he had been swung up into the air, his feet leaving the floor. He hung there grotesquely for a long moment as if held by invisible strings from the ceiling, arms hanging limply by his sides. Then his legs buckled under him as though no longer able to bear his weight and every bit of life seemed to go from his body as he crumpled into an inert heap on the floor.

Leaning back, Steve moved against the bar and stood there for a long moment, his shoulders firmly against it to make sure he didn't fall. Slowly, his head cleared and strength began to flow back into him. Silvers lay where he had fallen, unmoving, his head on one side, a trickle of blood still flowing from his nose. Around Steve, the place had become quiet. Then, out of the corner of his vision, he saw movement.

Swinging, he saw Carew pushing himself unsteadily to his feet, shaking his head. He remained on his hands and knees for a moment, then got up, grabbing at the nearby table for support. His wandering gaze finally fastened on Steve and he rasped thinly: 'I won't forget this, Marshal. You can be sure of that.'

Steve gave a tight nod. 'Don't try to go out of your way to rile me again,' he said quietly, his tone ominous. 'The next time you want to pull a gun on me, you'd better be ready to fire it.'

The banker glared at him angry and thwarted, then spun on his heel and strode to the door, pushing through it, out into the street. Steve looked after his retreating figure for a few seconds, then bent, picked up his hat and clapped it onto his head. Picking up Silvers' gunbelt, he placed it on the bar. 'Better give that to him when he wakes up,' he said sharply. 'And the next time, I'll use my guns instead of my fists on him. Better warn him.'

Leaving the bar, he thrust his way through the batwing doors onto the boardwalk and turned in the direction of the hotel. It was already dusk, the sun having gone down, turning the air blue and cool. The reds and oranges of the day had gone, and there were purple shadows lying over the street with the first yellow lights just beginning to show, in a few of the late-night stores and the windows of the hotel.

As he passed one of the narrow alleys leading off the main street, he heard the soft voice from the darker shadows.

'That you, Marshal?'

He paused, glanced down the alley but could make out nothing. 'Yes, who is it?' he asked thinly.

'I want to talk to you about the man who hired Benton to kill you.'

63

Steve hesitated, sucked in on his lower lip, then gently eased one of his Colts from its holster, checked that every chamber was full, then stepped into the alley. This could well be a trap. Maybe it was Carew waiting down there with a gun laid on him, just waiting for him to step off the street to drop him.

Cautiously, he moved deeper into the shadowed alley, eyes straining to pick out the faintest shadow. Then he caught a glimpse of the man standing by one of the low buildings, saw that the other held his hands well away from his sides, that he was too big to be the banker. Some of the tension left him, but there was still enough in him to warn him of danger a second before he heard the soft tread that sounded at his back. He half turned, knowing that the danger was not from the man in front of him, cursing himself for not having realised what a fool he was being. But he was not soon enough. Something crashed down on the back of his unprotected head and everything, the shadows, the faint shout of laughter from the street behind him, the tinny sound of the piano in the nearby saloon, all faded and he knew nothing as he pitched forward into a heap and a bottomless pit of blackness.

CHAPTER IV

A BEGINNING TO FURY

SLOWLY, Steve Enders opened his eyes, tried to focus them but for a long while it was impossible. Everything blurred and danced and there was a haze of pain inside his head, every breath he took, every beat of his heart sending a splitting spasm of agony roaring across the top of his skull. He lay there for several minutes, forcing himself to think properly. Screwing up his eyes, he managed to focus them, to stop the blurring dizziness. The sky over his head was pitch black now, a velvet backcloth on which the brilliant diamantine stars were studded in their thousands. There was no moon, but he guessed that it was late and he had been unconscious for some time.

Grunting with the pain, he forced himself onto his knees, knelt there swaying while his head cleared, ran his tongue over furred lips. Gingerly, he reached up and felt the top of his head. There was the stickiness of blood on his scalp and he winced as his fingers probed the wound. Whoever had hit had meant to keep him out for some time, although he doubted if they had meant to kill him. Had that been the case, they would have found it a simple enough matter while he had been out cold. A knife would have been quick and silent if they had not wanted to be heard.

He puzzled over that while he knelt there, not daring to get to his feet at that moment, until his head stopped ringing. Nothing seemed to have been taken. Even the gun which had been lying in the dirt nearby where it had fallen from his hand, was untouched. The slugs were still in the chambers. He thrust it back into its holster, finally succeeded in getting to his feet. Sickness swept over him, threatening to choke him and he clung onto the wall for support, swaying on his feet. His knees felt as though they had been turned to water, with scarcely any feeling left in them. With an effort, he staggered to the end of the alley, clung to the wall as he peered up and down the street. There were several horses tethered in front of the saloon, but no sign of anyone on the street or the boardwalks. Painfully, he made his way to the hotel, took his key from an astonished looking clerk and went up to his room, locking the door behind him. First he had to clean himself and then try to figure out the reason for that attack in the alley. Things had been happening mighty peculiarly that night. First that unprovoked assault on him in the saloon, and then the attack in the alley. He tried to let ideas run through his mind, but the dull, throbbing ache had returned to his skull and it made it impossible for him to think properly.

He poured water into the basin, washed his face and then dabbed at the blood on his head, wincing every time the cold water touched the wound, but it helped and at last, he was able to sit down in the chair beside the window, lighting a cigarette, drawing the smoke deeply into his lungs. His body ached from the battering it had received and every limb seemed to have been bruised in the fight with Silvers. At least, it hadn't been the big foreman who had attacked him in the alley; he felt certain of that. The other would have been still stretched out unconscious on the floor of the saloon when he had been attacked. Carew? It was possible. The other could have arranged for that other man to decoy him into the alley and he had then come up from behind and knocked him out with the butt end of a revolver.

He recalled the man whose face had seemed vaguely familiar, the man who had slipped out unseen and unnoticed when the fighting had begun. Little bits of the puzzle were beginning to slot themselves into place, he reflected, now that he was able to reason things out more clearly. He smoked the cigarette slowly, savouring it. It helped to ease the feeling of tension in him.

He had just finished the cigarette when he heard the sound of shouting down in the street, saw the group of men moving along the boardwalk, watched as they halted in front of the hotel. He recognised Blaine there and thought he saw Carew, the little pompous banker, but he could not be sure for a moment later, they streamed into the hotel and he lost sight of them from the window.

There was the sound of men coming up the stairs. Then they paused outside his door and he heard a man yell: 'He's in there all right, Sheriff. I saw the light in his window.'

A moment later, someone knocked loudly and insistently on the door. He waited for a moment, then Blaine's voice called: 'All right, Enders. We know you're in there. Open up unless you want trouble. You can't shoot your way out this time.'

Steve paused for only a moment then padded forward and opened the door. Sheriff Blaine rushed in, a drawn gun in his hand. He motioned Steve back into the room and behind him, more men came inside. Steve saw Silvers but this time the other had had time to sober up and come to his senses and he prudently stayed in the background, behind the man Steve had seen with him, the man whose face he had been before; bleak eyes watching him with a hint of amusement in them.

'You're showin' sense not tryin' to resist arrest, Enders,'

said the sheriff in a sarcastic tone.

'Arrest?' Steve stared at him. 'What's the charge, Sheriff?'

'Murder,' said the other tightly, 'as if you didn't know. I warned you what might be the consequences if you stayed in town, but it seems you didn't bother to take my advice. Now you're in real trouble.' He kept the drawn gun painted at Steve, not once relaxing his vigilance.

'What's this about murder'?' said Steve. For a moment, he thought he had not been hearing right, that the blow on the head had affected his senses. Then he saw the looks on the others' faces and knew that something had been framed against him, and for the first time he began to understand why he had been knocked unconscious instead of killed in that alley.

'As if you didn't know,' broke in Silvers from the doorway. His eyes were hard, narrowed to slits. There was a red smear of blood on his face and one eye was swelling, giving Steve a solid feeling of satisfaction. 'I figgered you for the kind to shoot a man in the back, particularly a man who was so drunk that he didn't know what he was doin' and who couldn't handle a gun anyway.'

'I don't know what you're talkin' about,' said Steve tightly. He swung his gaze back to Blaine. 'Just what is all this talk, Sheriff?'

Without answering, Sheriff Blaine came forward a pace, reached out and unbuckled Steve's gunbelt, stripping it off and holding it over his free arm. Then he said throatily: 'Carew, the banker, was shot in the back less than an hour ago, in the middle of the street. He never had a chance, but there are plenty of witnesses who saw you pull the gun on him.'

'That's a lie,' Steve snapped.

Silvers grinned viciously, lips curled back over his teeth. 'Ain't it natural that he'd say that to save his own skin. I saw you sneak up behind him and shoot him down. You sure weren't here in your room when we came lookin' for you

68

immediately afterwards. You must've been hidin' out some-where in town and then sneaked back here to pack before ridin' out.'

Steve swung on him. 'If I didn't know that you were stretched out on that saloon floor when I left, I'd say it was you who hit me over the head in that alley and left me out cold while somebody killed Carew so as to frame me for the murder.'

'You ain't goin' to get out of it as easy as that,' muttered Blaine. He stepped forward, moving around to the side of Steve, motioning with the gun in his hand. 'You'd better come along to the jail. We can ask any more questions in the mornin'. Right now, I'm locking you up on a charge of murder. Whatever the truth may be, it'll all come out at the trial.'

Steve's smile was strained and tight. 'You don't really believe that there will be any trial, do you, Blaine?'

'There'll be a trial,' said the other harshly. 'Now move along to the jail. I don't want to have to shoot you down in cold blood.'

'No better than what he did to Carew,' said a man from the doorway.

Steve walked forward, thrusting through the crowd in the passage, down the stairs and out into the street. His mind was whirling. Someone had laid this trap for him with a great deal of cunning, there was no doubting that. And he had walked into it with his eyes closed. That brawl in the saloon had all been part of the plan. There must have been twenty men there who had heard him threaten Carew, warn-ing him to use his gun the next time he tried to draw. And if this was backed up by more men who would swear they had seen him shoot down Carew in the back, there would be no chance for him to wriggle out of this.

Out of the corner of his eye, he saw Silvers grinning viciously on the boardwalk as the other stood to one side to let him pass. Very soon, word of this would get back to Marsden, if the other was not already somewhere in town.

Then a lynch mob, formed quickly and simply from the men in the saloons and he would be taken from the jail and strung up from the nearest branch. It was a common enough occurrence in these frontier towns. Before the circuit judge arrived, he would have been buried six feet deep in Boot Hill and almost forgotten by anyone.

'All right, inside!' snapped Blaine as they reached the jail. He thrust at Steve, grinding the barrel of the Colt into the small of his back.

They went to the rear of the building, where the cells opened out on either side of a short passage and Steve was hustled into one of them, the door slammed and locked behind him. Blaine stood eyeing him for a moment through the bars. In the distance, there was the sound of the crowd going back to the saloons for another bout of drinking and singing.

'Do you think I shot Carew in the back, Sheriff?' Steve asked thinly.

'Don't much matter what I think,' answered the other from the darkness. He rubbed his chin thoughtfully. 'I just see that the law is carried out. But I did try to warn you about this.' He picked up the lamp from the floor and moved off along the passage.

'One thing, Sheriff,' Steve called along the corridor, 'I'd appreciate it if you'd let me have somethin' to eat. Ain't had a bite all night.'

There was no reply from the other and a moment later, the door at the end of the passage was slammed hollowly and everything was in darkness. Steve glanced about him.

The cell was small and cramped, with only the single iron bunk along one side and a small, square window set high in the wall through which he could just glimpse the stars set in a portion of the sky. He reckoned that it was close on midnight and still the sound of drunken singing and yelling came from the saloons along the street. Maybe Marsden was there, firing the men with whiskey, telling them how good a

70

man Carew had been and that it was a damned shame that somebody should shoot him in the back like that, a coward's act, killing one of their most important citizens, and what were they going to do about it? Wait for the judge to come along in a month's time maybe, and then have him transferred to some other town for sentence? That way, he might wriggle out of it altogether. Better they should take care of it themselves and save the judge a job and the town a heap of money on a trial. The result was a foregone conclusion anyway. Why waste time? It would be so easy for an eloquent and persuasive man like Marsden, already held in high esteem in the town, to turn the heads of the crowd, particularly with a few of his own men discreetly placed among the others.

Cal Marsden stood on the small stage at the end of the saloon and waved a hand expansively in the direction of the bar. 'All right, lads,' he called, 'the drinks are on me tonight. Drink up all you can.'

He smiled broadly as he watched the men stampede towards the bar. Everything was going as he had planned. That marshal from Kansas was in jail on a charge of murder and Carew, his partner in the bank, was dead. He himself had always believed in killing two birds with the one stone whenever it was possible and this evening had been one of those occasions when it had worked out without a hitch. But the longer Enders was alive, the longer he would have to worry and so he was determined that the marshal would be taken from the jail that night and strung up just outside the town. That way, everything would be nice and tidy and nothing would reflect on him. There would still be Gantry to take care of, but with the marshal out of the way, he did not think that would be too difficult to arrange. As Blaine had so rightly said, although he had not agreed with him at the time, it had been a mite foolish bringing Enders to town. He should have foreseen that it could only mean trouble for

71

him. He had been stupid to think that the other would arrest Gantry on a murder charge without doing some questioning for himself.

Silvers came out of the crowd around the bar, moved up onto the stage. He rubbed his jaw tenderly. 'You figger the boys will take Enders from the jail when you give the word, boss?' he queried.

'Feed 'em plenty of whiskey and they'll do anythin',' said Marsden. 'I'll have a talk to 'em when they've drunk up.'

Marsden waited for five minutes, then stepped towards the front of the stage, holding up his hand for silence. There was a moment of muted conversation, then the saloon was quiet as the men turned to face him.

'All right, men,' he said loudly, so that his voice carried right to the back of the room. 'You all know me. I've lived here with you for nearly thirty years, so I figger I can rightly claim to be a part of Anderson, just as much as anybody. And it hurts me when some dirty, murderin' side-winder rides into town – even though I'll admit that I sent for him myself – and repays our hospitality by shooting down a man like Carew in cold blood and in the back.'

'Let's pay him back in full with a rope,' yelled one of the men harshly.

'Get him out of jail and string him up,' called another.

Marsden held up his hand again. 'I know how you feel, boys,' he said, 'but I ain't the law here. Sheriff Blaine is the law and we don't want any mob rule in Anderson.'

'You don't mean to let him stay there in jail until the judge gets here, do you, Mister Marsden?' shouted the first man. He swayed away from the bar and advanced into the middle of the floor. 'After all, Carew was your partner. You got more cause to want his killer punished than anybody here.'

A shout went up from the rest of the men in the saloon. 'We're wastin' time. I reckon Blaine will know the best thing to do if we all march in on the jail. He's no fool and he won't try to stop us.'

Some of the men at the back began to mutter threateningly. Cal Marsden threw a quick, appraising glance over them. They were getting worked up now, he reflected tightly. Very soon, they would be taking the law into their own hands and heading for the jail.

'All right, men, think it over,' he called, raising his voice to make himself heard above the muttering. 'In the meantime, there's still plenty of rye in the saloon.'

The men moved to the bar. Marsden turned towards Silvers. 'Give 'em another half hour,' he said confidently, 'and I reckon we can say goodbye to the marshal. Once that's been taken care of, we'll decide what to do about Gantry.'

Steve heard the shouts from the saloon as he lay on the iron bunk in the cell, knew what they portended. Marsden was there, for sure, stirring up the crowd in that gin mill, getting them into the mood for hanging, but staying in the background himself. Marsden was like that, he thought tightly. A man who wanted others to do his dirty work for him, not wishing to soil his own hands with murder. Just as he had brought him in, in an attempt to get rid of Gantry. He felt sure now in his own mind, that this was the fate which the other planned for Victor Gantry when the time came. A lynching mob, all steamed up, followed by a necktie party somewhere on the outskirts of town. And there would be no help from Sheriff Blaine. He was a man who turned away from his troubles, wanted no part of them, and he would run and leave the jail unguarded and possibly with the outer door unlocked, salving his conscience with the thought that no matter what he tried to do, one man could not possibly hold off a crowd of whiskey-incensed men like that and he could only get himself killed in the attempt.

He swung his feet to the floor and got unsteadily to his feet. He had never felt so utterly helpless in all his life. Reaching up, he grasped the iron bars set into the window and tested them, but they were solid and although he tugged until his arm and shoulder muscles cracked with the strain and the dull thumping ache came back into his skull he made no impression on them.

There was more loud talk from the saloon. For a moment, Steve felt a tiny rush of panic as he visualised them already moving out of the saloon, into the street and heading towards the jail. There was far too much noise out there, noise to drown the sound of men when they broke into the jail. If the usual routine was being adhered to out there, the men would be settling down soon to their last bout of drinking, before moving out in a body and converging on the jail.

He went over to the cell door, tried to see along the passage but it was pitch black. Then he caught a glimpse of the tiny strip of faint light which showed under the door at the far end and guessed that Sheriff Blaine was still there in the outer office, a troubled man, who did not wish to join with the revellers in the saloon. He wondered if Blaine had been taken in by this trumped up charge with which Marsden had succeeded in framing him.

He called out loudly: 'Hey, Sheriff!'

For a moment, there was no sound except for the faint echoes of his own voice rustling along the passage. Then the door at the end of the corridor opened and in the square of yellow light he saw the sheriff's portly figure framed in the opening.

'What is it, Enders'?'

'I'd like to talk to you.'

'For Pete's sake, go to sleep. You'll be able to say your piece in the mornin'. '

'Hell, this is important. And bring me something to eat and drink. Or do you usually starve your prisoners like this?'

The other muttered something under his breath, stepped back into the outer office, he left the door open and a little while later, he came back with a tray in his hands, grumbling hoarsely as he paused outside the door, unlocked it, then stepped inside, handing the tray over. He stood near the door, his hands close to the guns in his belt, eyeing Steve suspiciously.

Taking the plate, Steve gulped down the coffee. It was only lukewarm but it took away the foul taste in his mouth. He ate the chicken sandwiches which the other had brought, glancing unobtrusively at the other from under lowered lids.

'Sounds like they're havin' fun out there in the saloon,' he remarked casually.

'They usually do,' grunted Blaine. 'So long as they behave themselves, I don't bother about it.'

'And Cal Marsden. I suppose he's with 'em.'

'Very likely. But you won't be goin' out there, so there's no need for you to worry.'

'I'm just worried in case they're figgerirg on takin' me out of this jail and stringin' me up from a convenient branch. I've seen things like this happen too often not to be able to recognise the signs.'

'There ain't goin' to be anythin' like that happen here, not so long as I'm sheriff,' declared the other tightly.

Steve shook his head very slowly, bending to place the tray on the small ledge by the bed. 'You won't be able to stop 'em when they come, Sheriff,' he said thinly. 'There'll be more than you can handle and they'll—'

Without completing his sentence, he suddenly whirled, the metal tray held between his fingers. It struck the sheriff on the temple, knocking him backward against the door of the cell even as he tried to reach for his guns. Before he could regain his balance, half stunned by the vicious blow, Steve had yanked the other's Colts from their holsters, thrust one into his belt, then grabbed the keys.

'Back up inside, Sheriff,' he ordered tersely.

'You won't get far,' muttered the other harshly. He lifted his hands and stepped back towards the rear wall of the cell.

'I'll get far enough, and this will be a better chance than

that which Marsden is goin' to give me as soon as he gets that mob out there stirred up. Now unbuckle your gunbelt and kick it over here.'

The other obeyed reluctantly. Keeping a sharp eye on him, Steve bent, picked up the belt and buckled it on quickly. 'I figger you know that I was framed for this shootin',' he said quietly. 'Marsden wants me out of the way and he means to do it tonight.' He stepped forward, 'All right, Sheriff. Now turn around.'

'You're sure goin' to die when Marsden hears about this,' asserted the other as he took a step away from the wall. 'He'll hunt you down no matter where you try to hide. And it ain't no use goin' to the Gantrys for help. They'll be next on the list.'

'Just let me worry about that,' Steve said grimly. 'Turn!'

The other turned slowly, pivoting on his heels. There was the glint in his eyes that told Steve he would try to get the gun as soon as the other relaxed his vigilance. There wasn't much time, he reckoned. He laid the heavy barrel of the Colt across the back of the sheriff's skull and the other lost the use of his legs, pitching forward, his shoulders striking the stone wall of the cell as he folded in every limb and crumpled heavily to the floor.

Quickly, Steve made his way out into the short passage, locked the door of the cell behind him and tossed the keys into the cell across the passage before running quickly into the outer office. The yelling and harsh singing from the saloon reached a shrill and tuneless crescendo. He opened the outer door softly and peered out. Lights showed in every window of the saloon, but he noticed with a feeling of thankfulness that almost every other building along the street was in darkness. Once those men came streaming through the doors of the saloon, they would be temporarily blind after the harsh light inside. He edged along the front of the sheriff's office, moving away from the saloon. He needed a mount quickly.

There were two, tethered to the hitching rail about twenty yards from where he stood, but even as he noticed them, the doors of the saloon burst open and a crowd of men stampeded into the street, began to march in a body along the street. He moved quickly, his body still aching intolerably from the beating it had taken earlier that evening. But he forced himself to ignore the pain and the bruises, came out into the open where one of the alleys opened off from the main street and ran the rest of the way towards the horses.

Fumbling with the rope, he unfastened the nearer animal, leapt up into the saddle, pulling the horse away from the rail and into the street. Several of the men saw him at once. The night became alive with yells. A gun barked and then another. Vaguely, he heard a roaring voice that he recognised as Marsden's, shouting: 'It's Enders. After him!'

The shouting was taken up by the others. More slugs tore through the darkness around him and he crouched low in the saddle, bending over the neck of the horse as he rode swiftly out of town, heels flailing against the horse's ribs as he urged it forward.

More guns roared in the night at his back as the men raced for their mounts. Marsden's voice faded into the distance, but Steve guessed that he was still shouting orders to his men. The street at his back became alive with thudding hoofs as the first men saddled up and rode out after him. The pack was coming at a run and there was no time to turn in the saddle and try to fire back at them in the hope of slowing their pursuit.

There was a brief moment when the hoofs of his horse clattered hollowly on wood and he knew that he had crossed the bridge over the river. Then he rode up into the dark, tumbled masses of the rocks, feeling them close in on him from all sides, as the trail twisted and wound through the boulders. Branches of thorn reached out and tore at his arms and legs as he crashed through the thick vegetation. Gradually, his eyes were becoming accustomed to the pitch blackness of the night and the starlight served to give him a faint, quivering glow.

The dig of his spurs sent the horse plunging ahead. He could hear the sound of the pursuers at his back but they were still some distance away and he realised that he had built up a precious lead over them. If only he could hold on to it for a little way, he might be able to swerve off the trail once he got clear of these boulders and thorn bushes and give them the slip. Several shots blasted, but he knew that he had not been seen, the men behind him were counting on him having to stick to the trail at this point and they were merely firing along it into the darkness, possibly hoping that a lucky shot might bring him down. The nearest a slug came to hitting him was when one ricocheted off the rocks ahead of him and went screeching off into the distance.

The trail lifted through the rocks for more than a quarter of a mile, then it levelled off and began to dip downward almost at once. He gripped the reins tightly in his hands, peering ahead of him, trying to pick out the winding trail as it twisted and turned without warning. He came out suddenly into a stretch of exposed, open territory, reined his mount for a moment, pausing as he listened to the sound of pursuit. It was coming nearer, but the men were forced to slow their pace where the trail narrowed, allowing only two men to ride abreast. He pushed on for perhaps two hundred yards, then ran into tangled brush once more that slowed his progress. He could hear the others crashing behind him as they ran out of the rocks and into brush. Cursing and yelling, they were still close behind him and he knew he had not thrown them off his trail.

He swung north now, into rougher country, gave his mount its head for perhaps another quarter of a mile and then slowed, listening. The riders seemed to be continuing along the trail, for they were moving past him, heading west, hoofs pounding on the hard ground. He let his breath slowly ease from his lungs. Ahead of him was a small clearing and he rode down into it, letting the horse blow.

Even here, he knew he was not safe for long. Once Marsden realised that he had turned off the trail, he would backtrack and spread out his men, swinging around in a wide arc to trap him. Slowly, the shouts died out in the distance.

Cal Marsden rode angrily, peering into the darkness that lay on all sides of him, sending his mount forward at a cruel, punishing pace, knowing that he was pushing it to the limit, but caring nothing. Enders had somehow given him the slip, had broken out of that jail just as the men were going to get him. How he had managed it and what had happened to Blaine, he did not know, had not wasted time finding out. Instead, he headed for his horse and had called to his men to follow him. If Blaine had been killed or injured, that was too bad.

He ground his teeth in sudden impotent anger. He ought to have known better than to trust Enders to a man like Blaine. Now this damned marshal was on the loose and they had to find him before he managed to slip through his fingers again and probably warn Gantry of what was happening. Whatever happened, Enders would know now that Gantry was not the killer he had been expecting to find here. And if Blaine had talked, believing that Enders would give them no more trouble, the marshal might even know about those title deeds and how he had obtained them.

He paused, reining his mount on a low knoll of ground, straining his ears to pick out the drumming of hoofs in the distance which would tell him which way Enders had gone, for there was little doubt now that he had managed to swing off the trail somewhere and was probably heading north or south. But all he could hear was the crash of his own men as they hunted through the brush.

'Quiet! Hold those horses still!' he yelled harshly. A gust of wind caught at his words and whirled them away. Even when his riders did finally come to a halt and the clinging silence settled over everything, he could hear nothing. He swung in the saddle, motioned Silvers to come up.

'He's slipped off the trail somewhere,' he muttered grimly. 'We'll have to go back and spread out on both sides.'

'That ain't goin' to be easy in this darkness. If only there was a moon we might be able to spot him in this flat country.'

'There won't be a moon for another two hours,' said the rancher savagely. 'Get the men together and tell them what to do. Whatever happens, however long we stay out here, we've got to find him.'

'And when we do?' queried the other and there was a feral glint in his eye as he touched his chin tenderly.

'Then you can do what you like with him, so long as he's finished,' grunted Marsden.

'I get you, boss,' said the other tightly. He wheeled his mount, rode off to where the rest of the men were clustered in a milling group, fighting to keep their horses under control.

Turning, they cut back along the trail, riding more slowly now, pausing every so often to examine the ground underfoot for any sign that might indicate where Enders had turned off the trail and headed out into more open country.

The storm which had begun to blow up as he turned off the trail, hit Steve squarely as he rode over the low hills, always moving north. A deep stream cut across his trail and he forded it cautiously, feeling the horse breast the water as it creamed into foam over the smooth, treacherous stones of the stream-bed. As yet, he could hear no steady abrasion as he expected from his pursuers, but he reckoned that by now they would have discovered he was not ahead of them and they would have begun to backtrack, searching for any sign where he left the main trail.

The wind blew in strong gusts, hammering against his face, without rain yet but full of the dry dust, hurling it at his flesh, so that it silted in everywhere, cutting under his eyelids, scouring his eyeballs, filling his mouth and nostrils making it difficult for him to breathe. His horse was suffering too, yet he had to keep moving. If he stopped, tried to find a place where he could hole up for the night, they might come on him without warning, surround him, and then wait him out. He had no food and they would not have to risk their own skins to force him into the open.

Keeping his head bowed forward, pulling up the high collar of his jacket around his neck, he tried to shield himself as much as possible against the dust and sand blown along by the wind. Long, loose bundles of prairie grass were bowled along by the gusts, snagging around the horse's hoofs as it picked its way carefully forward. The going was tough now, really tough and in one or two places, he was forced to dismount and lead the horse forward through the rocks that studded the slope.

When the rain finally came, it brought a mixed blessing. It kept down the dust, but within moments he was soaked to the skin and the wind cut keenly through his clothing and his flesh, chilling him to the bone. But if it hampered him, it was sure to hamper his pursuers also and the rain would serve to wash away any tracks he may have made.

Shivering convulsively, he continued to ride, not knowing where he was headed, striving only to keep ahead of Marsden's bunch. They had the advantage that they probably knew this country well, knew all of the winding trails through the hills and could cut him off once they figured out which way he was headed. Marsden could even split his bunch, cover a wide area without too much trouble.

It was almost dawn when he heard the faint tattoo of hoofbeats in the distance. The faint grey streak of light just beginning to show in the east gave him sufficient light to see by and he rode to the top of a small, rocky knoll overlooking the plain below, peered out as far as he could see. At first, it was impossible to make out anything. Then he caught the slight movement in the distance, saw the small bunch of men, spurring their mounts in his direction, circling in from the west. The rain had stopped and they were dragging up a trail of dust which had enabled him to pick them out even before he could make out the individual riders.

Even as he saw them, he turned his head, looked in the other direction and thought there was movement there also. Thirty seconds later, he was sure, knew that Marsden had not waited once he had discovered his trail leading into the hills. He had split up his men, sent them circling round in a wide sweep so as to catch him when he came down from the hills. He voiced a muttered curse. All the time he had been riding, he had been fooling himself into believing that he was staying ahead of them, when in reality Marsden had proved to be too clever, too cunning for him. He had ridden neatly into a trap.

To his right, there was a wide canyon, dipping down towards the plains to the east. If he could make it along there without being seen, he stood a chance of crossing the next ridge out of sight of the nearer group of men and once they had entered the hills, possibly not thinking that he could have made such good time in the night, he could ride out and slip through the net in that direction. It was his only chance and there was no time to waste. Within twenty minutes, the first group would be in the low foothills, working their way swiftly along the trail to cut him off.

He gigged his tired mount, kept his head low, working his way towards the canyon. Now he could just make out the thunder of hoofs clearly. A minute later, he crossed a narrow cattle trail leading up into the hills, swung right and rode down into the cool darkness of the canyon. The sheer walls of rock closed in on him from both sides and in places the canyon became so narrow, in contrast to what he had seen from higher up, that his legs scraped painfully against sharp outcropping fingers of stone that tore at him. It seemed to take him an eternity to reach the far end of the canyon. When he did, pausing before he moved out into the open, there was, once again, the on-travelling murmur of horses being spurred to the fullest extent.

Risking a cautious glance around the wall of tapered rock, he made out the group of men sweeping in single file along the hill trail less than half a mile away. It was impossible to tell whether Marsden was with them, but he thought he saw the tall figure of Silvers, the Lazy Y foreman, with them, urging the men on. They moved deeper into the hills and the rocks swallowed them up. There was no sign of the other group of men riding in from the west and he guessed they would move up into the hills parallel with the other group, converging on the spot where they considered it likely he was.

Waiting for two minutes, he listened as the steady abrasion of sound died away into the tall hills, then gigged his own mount slowly into the open and rode down the trail to the plain before him, feeling a faint sense of relief in his mind. Down in the rough grass, he spurred his mount, riding away from the hills towards the grey flush of the early dawn. Now that the road had reached level ground he made better progress and as he rode, he found time now to turn over in his mind what his next actions should be. There was no doubt that things would be pretty hot for him if he ever went back to Anderson. Marsden would see to it that every citizen heard his version of the story and every man's hand would be against him. Blaine would probably have a posse out hunting him down, helping Marsden's men in the search.

A grim smile played over his lips as that thought went through his head. Here he was, a United States Federal Marshal, being hunted down like a common criminal by the people he had tried to protect, on a trumped-up charge.

He decided that the first thing he must do was to ride out to Gantry and warn him of what had happened. He guessed that Marsden would also reckon on him doing that and would deploy his men to cover the Gantry spread when they failed to locate him in the hills. He may even have sent some of his men to watch the trails into Gantry's spread. But that was a risk he had to take. The longer he was a hunted man, the more the advantage went to Marsden and it was up to him to reverse that trend, take the fight to the crooked rancher. And if possible, he had to discover what it was that the other was hiding.

CHAPTER V

ROUGH JUSTICE

When Steve finally rode into sight of the Gantry ranch, nestling in the deep valley, it was high noon and the heat head was a burning pressure over the land, a piled-up intensity that brought the sweat out on his forehead and mingled it with the dust already there so that it trickled down his cheeks in itching, irritating rivulets. He reined his mount on the edge of the hill that overlooked Gantry's place, let his gaze wander carefully in all directions. A thin column of smoke came from the ranch-house and curled lazily into the sky. A dozen or so horses stood drowsily in the corral and as he watched, he saw one of the hands move out of the bunkhouse and make his way over to the corral, where he pulled himself up onto the fence and seated himself there, hat tilted to the back of his head to keep off the sun's heat.

Moving forward, he circled the lush meadows, reached timber on the other side of the ranch and came in from the west. The door of the main house was open to let some of the heat out, but after the storm of the night there was now scarcely a breath of wind.

The man seated on the fence of the corral gave him an idle glance, then went back to his silent contemplation of the courtyard, lost in his dreams in the sun. Everything certainly looked normal here. But then, it would not be easy for anyone to get past Gantry's men. The man had lived a long time with the threat from his neighbour and although he, Steve, had ridden in, he had been let in, his passage through the meadows not going unnoticed. Had it been any of Marsden's men, they would not have been let through.

He swung dawn from the saddle, took his mount over to the corral and turned him loose, then made his way to the main house. Victor Gantry came out, gave him a brief smile. 'Heard you were ridin' in, Marshal,' he said in greeting. 'Come along inside. I'll get Beth to make up a meal for you.'

The girl came into the parlour a few moments later, eyed him speculatively for a moment, then said: 'You look as though you've been in trouble, Marshal. There's a bruise down your cheek and you seem to have been riding all night.'

He nodded as he sank gratefully into a chair, thrust his legs out in front of him. A deep weariness flooded through him and Gantry said quietly: 'Leave him alone for a while, daughter, until he's eaten. Then he can tell us all about it.'

The girl seemed on the point of saying something further, then stopped, turned and went back into the kitchen. Steve heard her handling the pans and plates and he placed his head against the back of the chair and half closed his eyes, aware that Gantry was watching him closely, saying nothing.

The smell of cooking reached him from the kitchen, making him realise just how hungry he was and how long it had been since he had eaten a good meal. He sat up in the chair as the girl came back, set the plate and cup of coffee in front of him on the small table by the window. Sighing a little, he set to work on the food, not looking up until the plate was clean and the cup had been filled with hot coffee for a second time.

Gantry waited for a moment, then said slowly: 'Reckon

you can tell us all about it, Marshal. Somethin' has happened. Was it trouble?'

Steve nodded. 'Marsden had some gunslick bushwhack me as soon as I rode into town. I had to kill him.' He glanced at Beth and he added: 'He was the leader of those men who attacked the stage. The trouble is that dead men tell no tales and there was no way I could prove it was Marsden who had hired him. The stage driver didn't recognise any of the bandits who tried to hold us up. I was hopin' that he might have been able to identify them as Marsden's men and then the rest would have been easy.'

'I guessed he would be at the back of it,' snapped Gantry. He got to his feet, paced the room for several moments before coming back and sitting down again in his chair. Finally, he said: 'I bet he didn't stop there once he discovered his plan hadn't worked.'

'No, he didn't. He put up that foreman of his, Silvers, and Carew, the banker, to start an argument in the saloon where there were plenty of witnesses. Carew tried to draw on me and I knocked him cold. Then Silvers tried the same and that's where I got this bruise. When I left the saloon, somebody called me into an alley and it was then that something hit me on the back of the head. The next thing I knew, it was about midnight and I was still lying in the alley. I got back to my room and hadn't been there more'n ten minutes when the sheriff and his men burst in and charged me with shootin' Carew in the back.'

Gantry nodded grimly, 'I can guess the rest.' He rolled himself a smoke. 'There'd be a lynching party ready to move in once the rest of the town was asleep.'

'That's right.' Steve noticed the look on the girl's face. 'Not a pretty thought,' he added.

'But the sheriff – ' she began.

Steve shook his head. 'He's a man who wants to forget his troubles. Once he'd locked me up that was the end of it as far as he was concerned. Maybe he manages to salve his conscience at nights, though I don't know how he does it. But he must've figgered I wouldn't risk it out on the streets with Marsden's men getting stirred up on whiskey, because he was a little careless when he brought me food. That's how I managed to get away, just ahead of Marsden's crowd. They'll be scouring the hills for me now. I spotted two bunches of them on my way here, but managed to give 'em the slip.'

'You'll be safe here,' said Gantry tightly.

Steve glanced at him quizzically. 'You think you're big enough to keep 'em out?' he asked meaningly.

'Nobody gets onto my land unless I give the word,' said the other soberly. 'I have men watchin' every trail into the spread. If Marsden tries to ride against me, I'll know it long before he gets in sight of the ranch.'

'And if he brings along the sheriff and a posse from town?' Steve queried.

'Then he may outnumber us, but he knows that he'll get as good as he gives and he'll lose so many men that he won't have a fighting force left by the time it's all over. That's why he's never tried to go up against me in the past.'

'Perhaps this time, though, he's got an added incentive to chance it.'

'Meanin' you?' The other raised his brows a little. He lit the cigarette, sat back in his chair. His voice was soft and gentle as he went on: 'He may want you badly, Marshal, but he won't risk everythin' just for that.'

'I hope you're right. At the moment, I need a little time in which to think and plan my next move.'

Beth began to clear away the dishes, carrying them into the kitchen. Steve could hear her rattling them in the sink as she washed and stacked them away. A riot of half-formed thoughts and ideas were chasing themselves around his tired brain. Gantry eyed him concernedly, then said: 'I reckon the best thing you can do right now, Marshal, is to get some sleep. You say you've been ridin' all night. You'll not be able to think clearly until you've rested.'

Steve nodded, tried to prevent his eyelids from going together. He got heavily to his feet, swaying a little from sheer exhaustion. 'You're sure that you can handle any trouble if Marsden does ride here?'

'I can handle it,' said the other with conviction.

In spite of the urgency that still filled his mind, Steve was forced to recognise the wisdom in the other's suggestion. He followed Gantry into the small guest room at the back of the ranch-house. The bed with its cool sheets looked tempting and he stretched himself out under them, feeling the linen caress his battered, aching body like a balm. Almost at once, he was asleep, his tired body surrendering to the weariness in it.

When he woke, it was grey dawn and he realised that he had slept through the afternoon and night. He dressed quickly, buckling on the gunbelt. Scarcely had he done so than there was a knock at the door and Beth Gantry came in with a tray.

'I was going to wake you,' she said quietly, 'You must have been tired. You've been asleep for nearly eighteen hours.'

'I've got a hunch that Marsden will know exactly where I am by now. He'll have searched those hills from one end to the other without finding me and soon he'll come ridin' here.'

The girl shook her head, but her eyes were troubled. 'I don't think he'll do that. I know the kind of man Cal Marsden is. He'll want to take things easy now that he's made two mistakes. He can't afford a third and riding in here with his men is going to be a big mistake. He'll have every trail out of here watched so that he can bottle you up here and know exactly where you are. That way he'll feel sure of himself and he'll know that you can't spoil any of his other plans.'

Steve pondered that, finally was forced to admit that it

made sense. 'I think I'll talk things over with your father,' he said finally. 'He may be able to help me.'

'You're not thinking of riding against Marsden?' There was a blend of surprise and concern in the girl's voice.

She looked at him wide-eyed. Yet there was a sudden lift of interest in her tone as she went on: 'You've got a plan?'

'At the moment, I'm not sure. I'm positive that Marsden has got somethin' to hide and if I could only find what it is, I may be able to use it against him. He evidently wanted me killed because he figgered I was getting a little too inquisitive about his affairs, once I'd switched my attention from your father to him.'

'It must have been something in his past,' the girl murmured, and said nothing for a long interval, apparently turning over the information in her mind. She led the way downstairs into the parlour. The room was empty, but through the open window, Steve glimpsed Vic Gantry on horseback riding one of the roans around the perimeter of the corral.

Gantry came in a few moments later, gave Steve a nod. 'Sleep well?' he asked, running a hand through his thinning hair.

'Far better than I've slept for some time,' Steve acknowledged. 'I've been turning things over in my mind, trying to work 'em out, but it isn't easy.'

'About Marsden?' said the other shrewdly.

Steve gave a brief nod. 'I'm sure there's something he doesn't want spread around town, but so far I haven't been able to find out what it is.'

Gantry's features bore a thoughtful stamp. For a moment he seemed cold and distant, lost in thought as he stared off into the distance, then he placed his powerful eyes on Steve.

'Only thing I can figger, is that it's connected in some way with the title deeds of those ranches he bought some years ago.'

'Title deeds?' Steve eyed the other thoughtfully.

'Cal Marsden wasn't always the big, powerful man that he is today, and there are some who reckon that he didn't come by the ranches he bought up, legally, but nobody was ever able to prove anythin' and those who sold out to him left for back East, or they just pulled out and nobody knows where they went. But we do know that Marsden was suddenly a big man in the territory, he had more land than anyone else and he'd bought a couple of saloons and the hotel in town, made himself a partner in the bank. He gave a lot to charity in town and you won't find many folk who'll talk against him. They reckon he's a fine, generous and upright citizen.'

'But you reckon there may be more to that than meets the eye,' said Steve musingly.

'I sure do,' growled the other.

'Now don't go making these wild accusations unless you can back them up, father,' said Beth from the doorway of the kitchen. 'There isn't a shred of evidence against him and unless you get something that will stand up in a court of law, you can do nothing.'

'Just how do we get a look at those title deeds, do you reckon?' asked Steve, interested.

'Won't be easy,' muttered the other tightly. 'Won't be easy at all. Ain't no doubt where they are though.'

'Where?' Steve's voice was harsh, explosive. Getting to his feet, he drew deep on his cigarette, felt a little of the tightness growing in his chest.

'Why in Chester, I guess.' Gantry looked up, swinging his gaze to Steve. 'Most all of the deeds are there in Lawyer Simon's office. But the way I heard it he figgered in on this deal, probably notarised 'em after Marsden had forced the ranchers to sign at gunpoint. You won't get him to talk.'

'No, I guess not.' Steve stared thoughtfully off into space, turning the new information over in his mind, assessing its possibilities. If there was any truth in Gantry's suppositions, it might well give him something on which to hang a case

91

against Marsden. The other would have undoubtedly covered his trail well; there wasn't much doubt about that and these papers would be kept securely locked away. Even then, even if he got his hands on them, unless either Marsden or the lawyer could be made to talk, he would have no proof that would stand up in a court of law that the deeds had been obtained illegally.

'You thinkin' of goin' into Chester to get those documents?' asked Gantry. He laid an inquiring glance on the marshal, clearly divining the trend of the other's thoughts.

'It's the only thing we can do,' Steve nodded. He drew in a deep breath of smoke. 'Not that the documents in themselves will help us much,' he went on practically. 'But if we do get them it may have the effect of forcing Marsden's hand and bringin' him out into the open where we can get at him, turnin' this thing around on him. A man who's jumpy will often do foolish things, maybe even give himself away.'

'Cal Marsden doesn't sound like an easy man to scare, from what I've heard,' said Beth Gantry from the doorway. 'And have you considered that he may already have guessed at your intentions? It's a long trail from here into Chester and there are a lot of places where a bunch of men can hide, ready to shoot you down from cover and the next time, they may not miss.'

Steve gave her a keen glance, arrested by the remark. It was a possibility he had considered and he knew there would be a lot of truth in it.

'Why stay in this quarrel now, Marshal?' she asked, not once taking her glance from his face. 'This is between my father and Marsden, something that has been going on for years. One other man can't make all that much difference to anything as big as this. If you were to ride on, Marsden might be prepared to take the middle trail and leave things as they are at the moment with an uneasy truce between us, knowing he can't hurt us without damaging himself and that we can do very little to hurt him.'

'Could be that I consider it part of my job,' said Steve, smiling a little. 'There are laws and there are men whose job it is to see that they're enforced. At the moment, the only law in Anderson is Marsden's. Sheriff Blaine is nothin' more than a figurehead. He does as Marsden tells him.'

'One man can't hope to change that,' persisted the girl. 'And especially a hunted man, already accused of murder.'

'Sometimes a man gets over-confident when he thinks he holds all of the high cards,' Steve told her. 'When that happens, he often makes mistakes. I figger that's what Marsden will do sooner or later.'

'But will you be alive to see it?'

'Stay out of this, Beth,' broke in Gantry. 'You've just got back from the East. There are ways here that you do not understand – evil ways. And if this country of ours is to grow, then they have to be stamped out. Someday, Anderson will be not a town, but a city. But that will never happen until we've driven men like Marsden and crooked sheriffs such as Blaine out of the territory.'

'And how many other men, good men, are going to be killed before you manage to achieve that?'

Gantry shrugged. 'You always have to make sacrifices for something if it's to be worthwhile,' he answered shortly. He turned to Steve, his eyes hard and speculative. 'If you're goin' to ride into Chester, I figger it'll be safer to ride at night. It's a long ride through the hills.'

Steve crossed the river that ran in a wide curve around the base of the range of foothills to the west of Anderson just as darkness was falling. The sun had gone down behind the towering crests of the mountains in a vast explosion of reds and yellows and the short twilight had come down quickly, throwing long shadows over the plains where the hills reared up on the close western horizon. The day's heat, held by the ground and released only slowly by night, still flooded around him, but the air was colder as he splashed his way through the slow-moving water and began the long climb into the hills. He had seen no other rider during the hour since leaving the Gantry ranch and this only served to heighten the tension in his mind. Pausing on the far bank, he listened intently. The wind, blowing down from the hills, brought with it the tag-ends of noise and his brows drew together as he considered the noise. Gently, he eased the long-barrelled Winchester in its scabbard then put his mount at the upgrade trail. He had a long way to cover before dawn and most of the trail lay through the tall, rearing hills where he would have to be on guard every second.

Darkness fell as he moved over one of the low ridges. Here and there, a lonesome pine thrust a tall, straight trunk up into the dark, star-shining heavens like a sentinel guarding the trails. By degrees the country roughened and became deceptive. The pines fell behind, gave way to stunted bushes and then to rough grass bordering the stony trail. He kept to the ridges that lifted almost directly above the stretching plains down below, not wishing to move any deeper into the mountains.

He did not know this country, had not ridden any of these trails before, yet he felt no concern for that. Most of his life had been spent riding hills like these. It had been a lonely and wandering life, following one trail to its end, only to discover that another began at that point stretching unknown before him. Being a lawman had its disadvantages. Never staying in one town long enough to put down roots and become an accepted part of the community. A man had to be fiddle-footed to keep a job like this for long, yet someone had to do it, ride the long frontier trails, keeping law and order in this newly-opened territory. And always, there was the danger. At first, it had given a certain spice in his task, but the novelty and the glamour of the marshal's badge had soon worn off; gunplay and danger were almost routine now.

When midnight came, he paused where a creek bubbled noisily across the trail, racing down from its source somewhere in the mountains, and a cluster of stunted trees grew out of the meagre covering of soil which lay over the rocks at this point. More whispers of sound filtered down from the ridges above him but he could see nothing in the dimness. He had the unshakable impression of men riding a host of criss-crossing trails all around him in the darkness and as he stood there, listening, the tension increased in his mind and body.

Hobbling his mount, he knelt beside the stream and drank his fill of the icy cold water, listening to the night sounds about him. The sky overhead was perfectly clear, the stars so brilliant and close that they seemed almost to brush his shoulders as he stood up, glancing about him. On the far side of the creek, the trail continued up into the mountains and he felt the whole crushing weight of them looming over him, blotting out more than half of the sky. From what he remembered there would be a moon later on in the night but until then he would have to ride with only the faintly shimmering starlight to give him light, a pale eerie glow that made the heavens overhead just a little lighter than the land, picking out the contours of the mountains in broad silhouette,

Mounting up again, he forded the stream, put the horse to the upgrade once more. As he rode the trail grew narrower, wound and spiralled in front of him so that he was eventually forced to rely on the animal instincts of the horse to guide him in places where his eyesight failed him altogether. Huge boulders, thrown up by some geological cataclysm long ages past overhung the trail, some seemingly balanced precariously over it, needing only the push of a fingertip to send them crashing down on him as he rode beneath them.

Then, at the very edge of his vision, one of the boulders did move. The movement was so unexpected that he was taken completely by surprise, delaying his instinctive, reflex actions almost too long. Then his knees drew together against the horse's flanks, raking the rowels of his spurs cruelly into the animal's flesh.

The horse responded instantly, hoofs striking the rocky floor of the trail with a metallic sound as it lunged forward. The boulder came crashing down the steep side of the trail in a shower of loose stones that pattered down onto his shoulders as he crouched low over the neck of the horse, urging every last ounce of speed from it. The roaring in his ears grew into a thunderous, cavernous sound which blotted out everything else. Then he was through and the tremendous weight of the boulder crashed onto the trail less than three feet behind him as they leapt clear.

He gave the horse its head for a couple of hundred yards where the trail ran on straight before him, then wheeled it sharply in to the side. Whoever had sent that boulder crashing down on the trail intending to kill him would undoubtedly follow him once they saw he had escaped and he had little chance of throwing off any pursuit on a twisting, treacherous trail such as this. Even in the daylight, it would be difficult; but at night, in the pitch blackness, where one false step would send them crashing over the edge of the trail, plummeting into the valley far below, it would be sheer suicide to attempt it. Flight was out of the question. He would have to stand and fight.

Sliding from the saddle on the run, grabbing the Winchester from its scabbard, he slid behind the rocks and waited, every nerve keyed, every sense alert. The muted echoes of the landslide started by the fall of the boulder were still bouncing across the valley below when he picked out the sound of horses moving cautiously from the rocks ahead. Then he made them out, riding in single file along a narrow fissure in the rocks; three men, obviously trying to push their mounts as quickly as possible. The first man's mount reached the trail and he swung its head sharply in

96

Steve's direction, then reined up until the others could come down, their horses sliding in the loose shale, forelegs straight, back legs buckled a little under them.

They knew he was waiting for them. Once they had missed the sound of hoofbeats fading along the trail, they knew as clearly as if they were able to see him that he was crouched down behind the rocks somewhere and they didn't intend to take any unnecessary chances.

Steve rested the barrel of the Winchester on the rock in front of him, sighted along it. The rider's head and shoulders came into the sights and he lowered the weapon slightly, then took up the first slack of the trigger. He heard the man mutter something to his companions, then turn and in that second, Steve pulled the trigger. The shot blasted loudly along the trail and the man suddenly threw up his arms as if trying to clutch at something invisible over his head, then pitched suddenly from the saddle as the horse reared at the sudden bark of sound with a shrill whinney of fear. The gunman's body hit the edge of the trail and then went over the side, crashing down the three hundred feet onto the rocky ledges below.

The other two men threw themselves out of their saddles, firing recklessly as they hit the ground and rolled back into cover among the rocks. Aiming carefully, Steve sent a couple of shots at the rocks, aiming not at the men, but placing his fire accurately in front of the horses. As he had intended, the ricocheting shots spooked the horses, sending them careering madly back along the trail. One of the gunmen, a dark, blurred figure, thrust himself to his feet, ignoring the danger from the hidden rifle, grabbed at the reins of his mount and tried to hold on as the horse stampeded.

His body was picked up and hurled with a savage, stunning force against the wall of rock, loosening his hold, and both horses continued their wild flight unchecked.

Swiftly, Steve pulled himself back into the shadows,

97

caught at the bridle of his own mount standing patiently nearby, thrust the Winchester back into its scabbard and swung lithely into the saddle, throwing a couple of shots from his revolver into the darkness behind him.

The shots dissuaded the gunmen from showing themselves. Without horses, it would be impossible for either of those gunhawks to follow him. There was no further danger from them now, but a new danger existed.

The thunder of those gunshots would have carried well in the darkness, crashing in rolling echoes through the hills and others of Marsden's men would know there had been trouble and would come riding for him, some doubtlessly riding ahead in an attempt to cut him off now that they knew almost certainly where he was.

He rode as swiftly as he could, always moving upgrade, further across the mountains. The tall peaks stretched away in front of him in an apparently never-ending succession, with long plateaux which, in places, smoothed out the steepness of the climb. An hour later, he crossed a rocky draw, noticed that the moon had risen, his view of it having previously been obscured by the towering peaks. It flooded the plains below with a ghostly glow and touched the rocks and rising pinnacles of stone, etched by wind and rain, with a cold, white radiance so that in places they seemed to be shining with a vague luminosity all their own. But in spite of its eerie quality, it gave him enough light to see by and he was able to make much better time than previously.

Once, he heard the brief, faint clatter of hoofs on rock a short distance away, reined his mount, leaning forward and placing a hand over its nostrils so that it would not give him away by any snicker at the closeness of the other horses. The riders went by at a quick trot less than two hundred yards away, below him, working their way back by another trail, moving in the direction from which he had just come. He picked up snatches of conversation as they rode by, an occasional harsh guffaw of laughter, the men utterly oblivious of his presence there.

He waited patiently until the steady tattoo of their horses faded into the uneasy, whispering quiet of the hills. Marsden would have all of his men out by now, searching for him, scouring every trail in the mountains, hoping thereby to block off every route down out of them and into Chester.

Whether he had already guessed at Steve's reason for heading in this direction was something he did not know. Marsden might believe he was merely trying to get away to save his own skin, hoping to slip out of the territory unseen. On the other hand, he was a very shrewd man and might even now be one jump ahead of him.

The way was upgrade for another three miles or so, and then he found the trail becoming more level, guessed that he was in the upper reaches of the mountains, no longer ascending. He began to breathe more easily. There was no sound of pursuit behind him and with the land growing gradually less rough his spirits began to rise a little. Two hours of this kind of riding and he felt that he had shaken off any pursuit for the moment and the only danger lay in any of Marsden's men lying across the trail which lay ahead of him. Reaching the point where the trail dipped down towards the distant plains, he paused for a moment to consider his position. If he delayed, there was the chance of them coming upon him again, possibly in force. If he took the trail on into Chester he ran the definite risk of being ambushed on the way. It was one of those snap decisions which had faced him on several occasions in the past, when he had been forced to weigh one risk against another. He turned down the trail and put his horse to a quick trot, letting it have its head. It was still fresh even after the distance they had covered during the night. His mind was still on the business of bringing Marsden to justice and yet from time to time, he found his mind wandering back to

Beth Gantry; a wilful, headstrong girl, yet with some of her father's gentleness and spirit about her. The thought, with its recollection of her face and the obvious concern she had expressed at his going out into the hills knowing that Marsden's gunmen would be looking for him, stayed with him as he rode out of the foothills and hit the main stage trail that led on into Chester, still some miles away. Now that he was out in the open, he felt a little easier in his mind. Here, although he could be spotted from a far greater distance than up in the mountains, he could also see his enemies while they were still far away and it would not be possible for them to ambush him or take him by surprise.

The feeling that Marsden and his men would soon try to swing round and box him in was strong within him, but by dawn, he was in sight of Chester, a blur of shadow on the horizon and there was no sign of any movement in the plains around him, Unless Marsden had ridden straight into Chester with a handful of his men to be ready for him there, he seemed to have outstripped them all.

He rode into Chester at sun-up and pulled up in front of the saloon. Until he knew how he stood here he did not mean to declare his intentions nor his reasons for being there to anyone. If the sheriff here was of the same calibre as Blaine back in Anderson, any approach to him would immediately be relayed back to Marsden by some means or another.

Going into the saloon, he found it open, but empty. After drinking up a sharp thirst, he called the bartender over. 'Any chance of gettin' something to eat here?' he asked. 'Anythin you can rustle up will do.'

'Sure thing,' nodded the other. 'Through there.' He indicated the door at the side of the bar. Steve went through, found himself in a small back room with three round tables, spread with cloths. A moment later, the bartender came in with a plate, eating utensils and set them down in front of him.

'Three eggs, bacon and beans do?' he asked.

Steve nodded. 'And hot coffee,' he said. 'Black.'

'You look as though you've been ridin' a long trail, mister,' said the other conversationally. 'We don't get many strangers in Chester riding in at this time of the mornin'.'

Steve glanced up. The other looked to be an honest man, not interested in bigger things. 'Any activity durin' the night?' he asked casually.

The other shook his head. 'Never heard of any,' he murmured. 'Nothin' much happens here unless it's a hold up of the stage. If the hill crowd get to hear of any payroll being moved out, they make a run for the stage.'

The other went out, was gone for perhaps, ten minutes, then came in with a heaped plate and a jug of coffee which he set on the table, then straightened, wiping his hands on the apron around his middle.

He stood there, just inside the doorway while Steve ate, spooning the food ravenously into his mouth. The scalding black coffee shocked some of the weariness from his body, acting as a stimulant to his tired mind.

'You know where I can find Lawyer Simon?' Steve asked without looking up.

'Ed Simon? Sure, about three blocks down on this side. You'll see the name over the door. Don't reckon you'll get him up for another hour or so yet though.'

'I can wait.' Steve poured himself a second cup of coffee, sipped it gratefully. 'Good coffee,' he said appreciatively.

'You got business with Simon?' asked the other. The bartender had a round, smooth face with watery blue eyes and a faint moustache just visible. No great amount of character showed on his features and Steve guessed he had just asked the question out of genuine curiosity.

'Depends on whether he's the right man to help me,' he said. 'I heard that he's able to witness signatures to documents, land deeds and the like.'

'Reckon so,' affirmed the other. 'He's the only lawyer in

town. He fixed up most of the ranchers around here when there was trouble with the Government over the old French and Spanish land grants. You ain't figgering on buying a ranch in these parts, are you?'

'Anythin' wrong with that?' Steve looked at him, sudden interest on his face.

'Well . . . no, I guess not.' The other rubbed his chin. 'But there ain't many bits of land for sale here and you'll get nothin' if you ride over the mountains to Anderson. Cal Marsden bought up most of the small ranchers there some years ago and there's only a fella by the name of Gantry still holdin' out on him.'

'But if there was any land, Simon would be the man to know about it?' Steve gave the other a tight, shrewd glance, uptilted the coffee pot until the last of the black-brown liquid was poured into his cup. He stirred in some sugar and drank the coffee slowly.

'I reckon so.' The bartender gave him a sharp stare. 'Sure you wouldn't like a room, mister? You look as though you could do with a few hours' sleep.'

Steve shook his head. 'Maybe when I've finished my business, I'll come back and take you up on that.' He got to his feet, moved out into the bar with the other close on his heels. There were a couple of swampers seated at one of the tables in the far corner, but that was all.

'Pretty slack at this time of the mornin',' he said, turning to the bartender.

'We don't get many customers until around noon,' admitted the other. 'Then more come in at night.'

Steve went out into the street. Chester was like most other towns in this territory. It had grown up over the years from a cluster of wooden buildings, thrown up hastily by men who had a vision, an urge to build, to start a community. Now it sat along two sides of the wide, main street which ran through the town and then out again into the desert which lay to the south and west.

He took his horse to the livery stables, saw that it had food and water, then walked along to the dingy office with Lawyer Simon's name in faded gilt letters over the door. Rapping loudly on it, he waited, casting a quick glance up and down the street. The sun was up now, throwing a warm red glow over everything, with long shadows lying over the street.

For several moments, there was no sound in the office. Then he heard the soft shuffle of footsteps approaching and a moment later, the door creaked open on a length of chain and a white face peered through the opening at him.

'Yes, what is it?' demanded a querulous voice.

'Lawyer Simon?' said Steve quietly.

'That's right. What do you want? The office isn't open yet, won't be for another couple of hours.'

'This is important,' said Steve harshly. 'I think you'd be well advised to listen to what I have to say.'

For a few seconds, the door remained half-open, then there was the faint rattle of a chain and a moment later, it swung open and the other motioned him inside. Simon was a short, wizened man with a gnome-like face and silvered hair making it difficult to tell his real age. He chained up the door behind him, then turned and led the way into a dingy office, the dusty windows reflecting a little of the sunlight that was just beginning to touch it.

'Well,' he demanded, 'what is it that's so important?'

'It concerns title deeds to certain stretches of land that were bought some years ago.'

Simon rose to his full, gaunt height, shook his head. 'I'm afraid that I don't understand. Do you wish to purchase some land around Chester? It won't be easy. I think I ought to warn you that most of the land has been bought and isn't for sale.'

'What about over at Anderson?'

Simon smiled thinly. 'I'm afraid the position there is even less encouraging than here. All of the available ranchland belongs either to Cal Marsden or Victor Gantry. I'm quite sure neither would consider selling any.'

'But surely it wasn't always like this? If things went here like they did most everywhere else, there would be a lot of small ranches, owned by more than a dozen families. How come there are only the two big men at Anderson?'

'That's quite simple,' went on the other smoothly. Clearly he suspected nothing, considered this to be merely an ordinary business deal from which, if he played his cards right, he might expect to receive a substantial amount for his personal services. 'You see, these people who came out here originally were not ranchers in the true sense of the word. They came looking for an easy way to make their mark in the world and when they discovered how difficult it was, the hazards they were called upon to face, they pulled up stakes and headed back East, discouraged by what they found. It was then that men who were able to withstand a bad winter, or any Indian raids on this territory, went ahead and expanded their own property by buying up the lands belonging to the smaller ranchers.'

'I see.' Steve rubbed his chin dubiously. 'I don't suppose I might see any of these title deeds, just to make sure there's no land I might get.'

Instant suspicion flared in the other's shrewd eyes. For a moment, he seemed on the point of making some sharp rejoinder, then he changed his mind, said thinly: 'I'm afraid that would be quite out of the question. All of the documents relating to purchase of property, title deeds and the like are kept locked away in the safe and are strictly confidential to my clients.'

'Perhaps this might change your mind.' Steve took out the badge from his pocket, held it out to the other, saw the instant change of expression on the lawyer's face, but the stubbornness still remained.

'So, a lawman.' The other's smile grew wintry. 'I somehow figured that might be the reason behind these questions. You don't look like a rancher to me.'

'I wouldn't let Marsden land you with everythin',' said Steve tautly. 'And that's what is goin' to happen. He won't take any of the blame for those title deeds that were got from these ranchers at gunpoint, and illegally notarised by you. When you both go for trial, he'll deny everythin' and those documents will be incriminating evidence as far as you're concerned. He'll merely deny all knowledge of them.'

'And you believe that you can bring Cal Marsden to trial on this charge?' There was a thin sneer of triumph on the other's features. 'You're not only wasting your time trying, but you're risking your life into the bargain. You're not in Kansas now, you know. Cal Marsden is a big man in these parts and you'll find it difficult to get out of the territory if he gives the word that you're making trouble for him.'

'I got through the cordon of men he threw around the trail to try to stop me from gettin' here.'

There was the same kind of look in the lawyer's eyes now that he had seen some time before in Marsden's. He thought about it for a moment before it came to him. Greed and a curious lust for power, that was it. 'You may not find it so easy to get out of Chester if Marsden should come riding here, looking for you.'

'I'll take that chance,' said Steve grimly. He went over to the door. 'And in the meantime, I'd advise you seriously to think over what I've said. There are a lot of things we can hang on Marsden. Be sure that he doesn't hang this on you.'

'I'm quite prepared to take that chance,' said the other grimly. He watched Steve closely as the other made his way along the short passage and out into the street. The chain snapped into place behind him as he stood on the board-walk.

He recalled that there had been a fine film of sweat on the lawyer's face and forehead when he had taken his leave and guessed that the other was not quite as composed, quite as sure of himself as he wished Steve to believe.

Glancing about him, Steve noticed the landmarks of the town which he recalled from the two days he had spent there before getting the stage into Anderson. On the face of it, both Chester and Anderson had many things in common. They had been brought into being at almost the same time, and because of this, because they had been started by men with the same dreams, the same ideals and thoughts, they had been built almost alike in every respect. The same main street that ran through each, with in this case, a secondary road that came in from the desert, ran across the main street close to the bank and the livery stables and then, curiously, lost itself in a maze of little alleys and back streets that ran around the rear of the buildings fronting onto the main street.

Slowly, thoughtfully, he made his way across the street, feet kicking up little spurts of dust. He was almost at the other side when he picked up the unmistakable sound of riders heading into town from the east. Swiftly, he ran into the shadow of the boardwalk, thankful for the wooden over-hang here which gave him plenty of protection and made it difficult for anyone to see him from the street.

Thrusting himself well back against the wall of the build-ing behind him, he watched as the tightly-bunched group of riders swung into view at the far end of the street and rode quickly along it, finally reining their mounts in front of Lawyer Simon's office.

Steve felt no thrill of surprise as he recognised the first two men to dismount and move towards the building. Cal Marsden and Silvers, his foreman. They had wasted no time in getting here when they had discovered he had slipped through their fingers in the mountains. And judging from the fact that they had come to the lawyer's place first, before even stopping off at the saloon, made it pretty certain they guessed where he would have been riding once he arrived in Chester.

Simon's face appeared at the window, he must have seen them ride up and a few seconds later, the door opened wide and they went inside. The rest of the men remained mounted up, their horses lathered in sweat, their clothing smeared with dust. They looked tired and hungry and one or two motioned with their hands in the direction of the saloon, but the tall, dark-haired man who seemed to have been left in charge shook his head emphatically.

Three minutes later, the door of the office opened and Marsden came rushing out with Silvers close on his heels. 'He's in town, boys,' he called loudly. 'He came here less than ten minutes ago. Spread out and search for him. He can't have got far.'

Steve pressed himself more tightly against the shadowed wall. He didn't have much time to get under cover. Already, the men were swinging down from their saddles, fanning out. He slid around the corner of the building, into a narrow alley that divided it from the next and turned and ran as quickly and noiselessly as he could along it. There was a vague shouting from the street he had just left. Instead of continuing to run when he reached the end of the alley, he ducked out of sight behind the low, broken wall, keeping his head well down.

He did not have long to wait. The lean gunman appeared at the far end of the alley, threw a swift, all-embracing glance along it, then began to move quickly forward, a gun in his right hand, his eyes alert for trouble. The sunlight behind him threw his shadow in front of his body. Steve's hand was on the barrel of his Colt, holding it reversed, as he tensed himself. He held his breath and let the man draw level with him, then go on for another two paces before he made his move. The gunman was peering along the passage to his right and did not even see the butt of the gun that crashed down, hitting him a stunning, slashing blow on the side of the head just behind the ear. The impact knocked him clean off his feet, sent him pitching forward, sprawling full length on the ground. The purely reflex action in his body brought the gun in his hand upward, moving in Steve's direction, but there was no longer enough strength in his finger to press the trigger and the gun fell from his nerveless hand, clattering to the ground.

Steve glanced quickly along the alley. There was no one in sight. Swiftly, he bent, thrusting the gun back into his holster, then caught the other around the ankles and dragged the inert body out of sight behind the wall and waited. A long moment passed, then he heard the sudden yell from the street. 'Jake! You found anythin' down there?'

When there was no answer, Steve heard the other moving cautiously along the alley, picking his way over the piles of rubbish which lay here and there. This man would not be so easy to take by surprise, he reflected grimly, he was already suspicious and doubly cautious and that made him doubly dangerous.

He held his breath in his lungs until it hurt, aware of the hard thumping of his heart against his ribs. He heard the harsh scrape of boots on the hard ground as the man shuffled forward.

'You here, Jake?' muttered the other once more. Cautiously, Steve lifted his hand, holding the gun ready for another clubbing blow. The man reached the end of the alley, held himself back obviously wary of any possible attack. Then he took a single step forward, peering about him swiftly. He glimpsed Steve moving in at precisely the same second that the gun began its downward swing. With a wild cry of alarm, he stepped back and flung up his free hand in an attempt to ward off the blow. It struck him on the shoulder as he half turned, numbing his arm, but doing little other damage. Savagely, Steve lashed out with his boot, his back and shoulders braced against the wall, caught the other a bone-cracking blow on the shin that sent him reeling back off balance. The other opened his mouth to yell another warning, louder this time to warn his companions in the street, but the sound died in a strangled gurgle as Steve struck him swiftly across the throat with the edge of his left hand. Gasping for breath, neck muscles corded and straining for air, the man tried to suck air down into his heaving lungs, temporarily unable to defend himself and once more, the gun in Steve's hand slashed down and caught the other a savage blow behind the ear. He dropped without a further sound.

Reaching down, Steve dragged the second man in beside the first. A quick glance told him that he had not been seen. Turning the men over on their faces, he pulled up their arms behind them and tied them securely with the bandannas taken from around the men's necks. Then he used their leather belts to hobble their feet.

Finally satisfied, he stood for a moment, looking down at them, sucking air into his body, breathing deeply from the exertion. Both men were unconscious and likely to remain that way for some time. A lump was beginning to rise on the first man's skull, but their pulses were both beating strongly. He felt neither anger nor satisfaction at what he had done. He cared nothing for either man. Had the positions been reversed, they would undoubtedly have shot him down without compunction.

For another minute, he remained there. No other sounds came from the end of the alley and he felt reasonably sure that the rest of the men were checking other roads in town. Marsden would also have to post some of them along the trails leading out of the town, and that would have the effect of depleting the force he had to search the town itself, but he was probably not worrying too much about going from one building to another hunting him down so long as he could be certain that he could not get out of the town. Trapped in Chester, it would be only a matter of time before he was found and Marsden might well consider he had all the time in the world for that.

He resisted the urge to run. A man running on strange and unfamiliar ground not only made far too much noise, but attracted attention. Whatever happened he had to find some place to hide until the night. He had no chance at all of getting out of the town during daytime. His only chance would be after dark. And there was also something else he had in mind. He needed those title deeds which Simon had already admitted were locked away in the safe in his office. He did not mean to leave Chester without them and the only chance he had of getting them would be to force Simon to open that safe at gunpoint. He had one advantage in that neither Simon, nor Marsden, would expect him to be so foolish as to try to go back there.

At the end of the alley which ran across the first he noticed the tall, abandoned building which thrust itself up from among a cluster of smaller wooden buildings, obviously stores which had been erected when the town had been brought into being, and which had long since fallen into disuse. Windowless and doorless, the two-storey building might be one of the obvious places for Marsden's men to search but—

His thoughts coagulated in his mind. It came so suddenly, this warning he got, was so close to him, that his nerves vibrated within him like the plucked strings of a violin. He sank slowly to the ground, careful not to make any quick movement that might draw attention to him. The three men came into sight less than fifty yards away out of one of the narrow streets and moved towards the empty buildings. From where he lay, Steve was able to watch as they went inside, vanished from view for several moments, being seen intermittently whenever they passed behind the open windows and doors. They were clearly searching every building intently, missing nothing.

By the time they came out again, they were all evidently satisfied that he was not hiding there. One of the men laughed, said something to the others, wiping the back of

110

his hand over dry lips. For a moment, they paused and debated among themselves. Then they turned and moved off into the direction of the main street and – Steve guessed – the saloon.

He waited, tensed and keyed-up, until he felt sure they were out of sight, then moved over to the tall, two-storey building, slipping inside the broken, shattered doorway.

There were still thin splinters of glass in the window frames, he noticed, catching the rays of the sun, sending painful flashes of light into his eyes. Glancing up quickly, he noticed the stairs leading to the upper storey and reckoned that from up there, a man might be able to look out over most of the houses and stores in the neighbourhood and see most of the town, could watch streets from angles that it was not possible to see from street level.

The musty smell of the abandoned place came up to him, assailing his nostrils sharply as he drew in a deep breath, peered about him in the gloom. Dark shadows still lay in the corners where the sunlight never reached and dust lay thickly on the stairs leading up to the other floor. He picked his way carefully up the stairs. Something scuttled into an unlighted corner and a pair of reddish eyes glared balefully at him from the shadows. Another rat ran across the floor above his head, producing a scurried, gritty sound that grated oddly on his taut nerves. These were the only sounds in the whole of the building. Now that those men had searched this place and found nothing, they would not be back in a hurry and he would be as safe here as anywhere in the whole town. The dust dragged up by his feet filled the air and he went further into the large room at the top of the stairs,

There was a pile of straw and wood shavings on the floor in one corner, close to the open, shattered window that looked down over the nearby streets and after making certain that there was no one in sight below, he stretched himself out on the straw, lay on his back, staring up at the ceiling of the room over his head. The warm air flowing in through the broken window made him feel drowsy, realising just how tired he really was after that long ride of the previous night along those interminable, twisting mountain trails. Taking one of the guns from its holster, he placed it on the straw within each reach of his hand, closed his eyes and went to sleep, surrendering himself to the utter weariness and exhaustion that pervaded the whole of his body.

What finally woke him was the light of the setting sun shining directly onto his face. He stirred briefly, then opened his eyes and forced himself awake, aware of his position. He had slept through most of the day, which was far longer than he had intended and a little chill went through him as he realised just how dangerous that had been. At any time during the long afternoon, Marsden might have sent out his men to check over every place they had searched that morning, knowing that he must have gone to ground somewhere, that it was doubtful if anyone had given him cover and he could not have got out of town without being seen.

He rubbed the sleep from his eyes, swung his legs to the floor and got to his feet, moving over noiselessly to the window and peering out. For a brief moment, the brilliant red rays of the setting sun, dipping rapidly now towards the mountains, blinded him and he could see nothing beyond the red-blue haze that danced in front of his vision.

Gradually, his vision cleared and he was able to make out the narrow alleys below him, and beyond them, over the roofs of the abandoned stores, the main street stretching across his vision from right to left. He could only make out the far side of it but there seemed to be plenty of activity going on down there although how much of it was just the normal supper crowds, making their way into the hotels and saloons, he did not know.

Thrusting the gun back into its holster, he crouched down by the window, feeling the pangs of hunger in the pit of his stomach, and the thirst that had cracked his lips and parched his throat and mouth. There was no chance of getting either food or water until after dark, he knew. Until then, he would have to bear the discomfort as best he could and keep a close watch on what went on below, him.

Darkness came down quickly once the sun had set. Within minutes, it seemed, the shadows had drawn themselves among the buildings and the first stars had appeared in the clear heavens, dim at first, but brightening and growing sharper as the sky around them darkened until it was like a stretch of black velvet.

In the distance, he picked out the sound of shouting and singing from one of the saloons, and then the tinkling of the inevitable piano. After a few moments, there was the sound of a woman's voice singing, her lilting notes lifting high into the clear air and reaching him easily over the tops of the low buildings.

By now, most of the townsfolk would be in the saloons or the hotel having supper, he decided; and it was almost time for him to move. If he waited too long, until everyone was off the streets with the exception of Marsden's men, he would be spotted at once, but now, with plenty of folk abroad, in the darkness he could pass virtually unnoticed.

Easing the guns in their holsters, he made his way cautiously down the rickety stairs, feeling his way carefully in the dark. At the bottom, he paused to glance about him, then went cautiously to the open doorway and peered out.

Nothing moved in the shadows, nothing disturbed the solemn stillness, and he edged out of the building, angling to the right, detouring to gain extra cover. Using what concealment there was, he moved along the alley, until he came out onto the main street. He had to chance Marsden having put a man on watch outside the lawyer's office. If he had, then the other would have to be taken care of; and Steve was relying on Simon being there, even at this hour of the night. He had the feeling that he had scared the lawyer

113

more than the other had cared to admit and until he was caught, he reckoned that Simon would prefer to remain in the comparative safety of his own office, rather than run around in the town, not knowing when Steve might meet up with him.

Now that he had reached it, the street seemed strangely quiet. Several horses stood patiently along the wooden rails on either side and here and there, a couple of men were in the shadows of the boardwalk outside the hotel, smoking quietly. He could see nothing of the men themselves, but the bright red sparks of their cigarettes were clearly visible in the warm darkness, waxing and waning in brightness as the men drew on them.

He had the feeling of suspense in that quiet stillness, almost as if the whole town were watching and waiting, wondering what was going to happen next, aware that something was about to break. Marsden's men, except for those staked throughout the town and on the trails leading out, would be in the saloons, standing along the bars drinking, or playing at faro or poker. He didn't know how soon Marsden could get them into action if it came to a show-down. His gaze flicked towards the sheriff's office. There was a lamp burning in there, showing clearly through the window. Was Marsden there, talking this thing over with the other, just so that when they did catch him, anything that was done, would be all legal and above board? If he was shot or hanged, and news of it leaked out, there would undoubt-edly be trouble over the killing of a marshal, and they would have to have a good story cooked up.

A group of men came from the nearby saloon and moved slowly across the street and Steve, acting swiftly, moved out so that he moved parallel with them and they passed between him and the men seated in the shadows on the other side of the street. He did not realise, until he reached the far boardwalk safely, that he had been holding his breath in his lungs all the way over. He let it go through his nostrils in small pinches. Sound of loud talk and the tinny beat of the piano came muffled to Steve from the saloon.

The nearest horses were tethered several yards away and one snickered softly as Steve moved in close to the side wall of the lawyer's office, keeping well into the shadows.

As he started to edge into the narrow passage, a man came out of the saloon, stood on the edge of the boardwalk, teetering on his heels as he stared along the street suspiciously. Hardly daring to breathe, Steve stood absolutely still, one hand on the gun at his waist, determined to sell his life dearly if the man did succeed in picking him out against the shadows. For what seemed an eternity, the man stood there, staring into the darkness. Then he pulled a tobacco pouch from his pocket and built himself a smoke, striking the match on the wall at his back, lighting the cigarette and pulling the smoke into his lungs before turning and going back inside. Once again, the night was reasonably quiet.

Cautiously, Steve edged his way around to the rear of the office building. In places, the passage was so narrow that he could only just push his way through it. At the back, he found a small courtyard, filled with boxes and barrels, lying around in a totally haphazard manner. There was a window close to the rear door and he tried it carefully when he found the door itself to be locked. There had been a faint light in the front window and he guessed that his supposition that Simon was hiding there was correct. If that was the case, it made his task a little easier than otherwise. He felt bitter at himself for not having forced the issue that morning. Had he done so, he might have been well away from Chester by now and with those vital title deeds tucked in his pocket.

The window was not locked and within seconds, he had opened it silently, revealing just enough space for a man to crawl through. The rough wood of the frame caught at his middle as he wriggled inside, reaching out with his hands to feel his way. Something hard came under his questing fingers and he recognised a wide table set almost directly under the window. Scarcely able to believe his good fortune, he eased his body onto it, making no sound and a moment later, he was standing inside the room, peering about him in the almost pitch darkness, striving to see. He set one foot forward and down with caution, testing the floor. A loose board creaked under his weight and he stood stock still, listening, but there was no sound from further inside the building, no indication that the sound had been heard. Another half dozen paces forward and his outstretched hand encountered the far wall of the room and he felt along it until he found the door. Twisting the handle gently, he opened it, passed through into a narrow passage, at the far end of which, was another door with a faint strip of yellow light showing clearly from beneath it.

Now that there was faint light by which he could see he reached the door in a couple of strides, pressing his ear close to it, listening for any sound from beyond it. For a long moment, he heard nothing. Then there came the sound of a chair being scraped back, followed by the soft sound of footsteps as someone moved across the room. Then there was the unmistakable sound of the shutters being put into place across the window facing the street. Steve waited until he heard the other go back to his seat, then pulled the gun from its holster, turned the knob of the door and stepped into the outer office, levelling the gun on Simon's body as the lawyer whirled in stunned surprise, his hand dropping instinctively towards a drawer of his desk.

'Try it,' said Steve quietly.

The other froze, then slowly lifted his hand, placing both of them on top of the desk. His face paled a little as he stared up at the marshal.

'I suppose you know that there are men all over town looking for you,' he said thinly. 'And every trail out of Chester is blocked. Better give yourself up and save a lot of unnecessary trouble.'

116

Steve shook his head slowly. He grinned at the other's obvious discomfiture. 'You've got me all wrong,' he said tightly. 'This is the last place that Marsden or his men will think of looking for me. Besides, I've come for those title deeds that you keep locked away in your safe.'

'If you think I intend to let you have them, you're crazy.'

'Don't try to be a hero.' Steve made his tone deliberately rough. 'I'm not here for fun. All you have to do is open that safe and get those deeds for me. Otherwise, I may have to use this gun and if you think I won't, just remember that I have nothin' to lose.'

'You're a lawman,' said the other. His eyes were like those of a hunted animal now, flicking from one side of the office to the other as if seeking some avenue of escape and finding none. 'You wouldn't shoot down a man in cold blood just because he refused to open a safe.'

'I wouldn't make any bets on that.' Steve moved forward, jabbed the barrel of the gun into the other's ribs. The man howled thinly, tried to back away, to get to his feet, almost falling from his chair in his effort to stand up. All of the colour had been drained from his face.

'You know damned well that those deeds won't help you, even if you do get your hands on 'em,' went on the other quickly, the words falling over themselves as they spilled from his lips. 'You'll never be able to prove anything with them.'

'Could be that Marsden will go to any lengths to get 'em back once he knows they're in my hands,' snapped Steve. 'Now quit stallin' and open that safe, or you'll soon discover whether or not I'm bluffin'.'

The other backed away until he was pressed up hard against the wall. Steve eyed him coldly, wishing that he could just pull the trigger now when it was safe, get the keys of the safe from him, and then get away. But that kind of killing wasn't in him, although the other was not to know that. Almost casually, he lifted the gun and brought the gunsight down across the other's face. It broke the flesh, drawing blood, and Simon staggered back, one hand going up to his cheek, staring down at the smear of blood on the back of his hand.

'Now I don't aim to ask you again,' Steve said ominously, his voice glacial with menace. 'I'll count to three and then pull the trigger.'

'They'll shoot you down before you get clear of the building,' said the other in a sort of gasp.

'One . . . Two . . .'

His finger tightened on the trigger, the knuckle standing out under the flesh. Simon's eyes were glued to the gun now, staring at the round hole of the barrel that was laid on his chest. His tongue moved over his dry lips and there was fear showing clearly at the back of his eyes.

'All right.' Somehow he got the words out. 'Don't shoot.' He moved away from the wall, bent to open a drawer in the desk.

Steve moved with him, his free hand reaching out and clamping tightly on the lawyer's wrist as he opened the drawer. As Steve had suspected, besides the bunch of keys in the drawer, there was also a small, snub-nosed automatic. He removed it carefully and thrust it into his belt. 'Another trick like that and I'll kill you,' he said tightly.

Simon took the keys, edged around the desk and went over to the large safe on the far side of the room. The sweat was running down his face and he no longer had his confident look. It seemed to take him longer than usual to find the right key, as if he were stalling for time, and Steve jabbed the gun into the small of his back, putting his weight behind it so that the other yelped with agony. At last, he had the door open, revealing a mass of papers and legal documents.

'Right,' said Steve. 'Get out those pertainin' to the ranches that Marsden bought up.'

The other riffled through the documents at the rear of

the safe, finally brought out a tight bunch tied with a piece of white ribbon. He held them out to Steve. Glancing clown at them, Steve was able to make out Marsden's signature on most of them, also Simon's, and witnesses to the transaction. Satisfied, he thrust them into his jacket, buttoning up the front.

'That's better,' he nodded. 'Now lock the safe again.' The other did as he was told. Stepping away, he had his back to him for a moment and Steve swiftly reversed the gun in his hand, hit the other without too much force across the back of the head. The lawyer crumpled to the floor without a single murmur. Bending, Steve pulled the inert body out of sight behind the desk, then moved back towards the other door. Scarcely had he reached it than he picked out the sound of heavy footsteps on the boardwalk immediately outside the shuttered window and a moment later, there came a loud knocking on the outer door and a loud voice called: 'You in there, Simon?'

When there was no answer, the man called again, more harshly this time, then tried the door, twisting the handle several times. Steve waited until he heard the other move away, pause, then hurry on more quickly as the man obviously realised that there was something wrong. Very soon, he would return with Marsden and probably some more men and break in the door.

There was no need for silence now. Swiftly, Steve made his way along the narrow passage, into the back room, and lifted himself up onto the table and squeezed through the window, cutting back through the alleys, heading away from the main street. Swinging round in a wide sweep that would bring him on the other side of the saloon from the lawyer's office, he came out into the main street again, noticed the shouting and running that went on some distance away, guessed that Marsden had been fetched from the saloon by his man and was on his way to the lawyer's place to see for himself what had happened. Steve waited for only a few moments, then moved towards the livery stables. A boy drifted from out back, glanced at him without any curiosity.

'Seems to be a lot of ruckus goin' on down there,' he remarked.

Steve nodded. 'Sounds like a drunken brawl to me,' he said casually, 'You got a horse I can have?'

'Sure, I guess so.' The other led the way into the stables, towards the stalls at the back. 'There's been plenty of men runnin' around town like dogs with their tails between their legs,' he went on. 'Wish I knew what it was all about. Regular livery man is away for a meal and I guess he'll be stayin' there to see what's goin' on. I'll be lucky if I see him again much before midnight.'

'That's rough,' Steve agreed, commiserating with the other. He pulled a roll of bills from his pocket, peeled off enough for the horse and a couple for the lad. The other took them with a look of surprise on his face, mumbled his thanks.

Riding flat over the saddle horn, Steve ran the big bay full out, rode through the entrance of the stables into the street, headed away from the noise nearer the centre of the town, a dark shadow, moving too quickly for any of the men outside the lawyer's office to see him clearly. The wind had risen, coming in sharp gusts that sent the balls of cactus and prairie grass bowling along the street, picking up the dust and whirling it around him. He wondered where the men guarding this particular trail would be. As like as not, they were trying to get some shelter from the wind and Steve had already noticed that the wind was blowing into his face, would carry the sound of his mount away from anyone watching the trail.

After several moments, he left the last of the buildings of the town, cut out towards the hills. There was no pursuit from behind and he rode slowly and carefully now, eyeing the darkness ahead, keeping his eyes alert for the first sign of any movement. The bay picked its way forward for several more minutes and then gave a tiny snicker of sound through its nostrils. The sound would not be carried far in the wind but Steve knew that his mount had smelt the presence of other horses.

Reining in to the side of the trail where it twisted and wound in a series of steep turns, he dismounted and led the animal forward on foot, keeping one hand over its nostrils so that it might not give him away. The men watching the trail could not be far ahead now. They moved through the brush that bordered the trail, swinging off it a little, then moving parallel to it. Steve saw nothing in the pitch blackness, but a moment later, borne on the wind, came the sound of a horse stomping on the hard ground and he froze instantly. Leading the bay off to one side, he tethered it to a short stump that grew straight up from the ground, then moved back towards the trail, keeping himself low, taking care not to make any sound that might be carried to the watchers among the rocks near the trail.

CHAPTER VI

SIERRA GUNS

Cal Marsden had been drinking in the saloon, content in the knowledge that wherever this marshal was, he could not get out of Chester alive; every trail, every route out of the town was covered by his men and he still had a handful searching all of the empty, abandoned shacks and stores on the eastern edge of the town. He felt reasonably certain that sooner or later, Enders would make a mistake and that would be the end of him. In the meantime, he was content to leave it to his men to smoke the other out.

It was at that moment that the doors swung open and one of his men burst into the saloon, cast about him for a moment, then came over.

'There's somethin' wrong at that lawyer's place, boss,' he said harshly. 'I thought you warned him to stay there until we'd caught up with that marshal.'

'That's right, I did.' Marsden swung on the other. 'What's happened?'

'There was no answer, then I knocked and the door is locked.'

'Damn.' Marsden heaved himself hurriedly from his seat, started for the door. 'Get the boys together and follow me. This could be serious.' His voice held a savage note.

Storming outside, he strode along the boardwalk to the

lawyer's office, pausing in front of the outer door. For a moment, he stood there, waiting impatiently until the rest of his men came pouring from the saloon. Then he drew his gun, hammered sharply on the door with the butt. There was no sound from inside the office, although he could just make out the pale yellow glow of a lantern around the edge of the wooden shutter which had been put up from the inside.

'He's in there somewhere,' he shouted. 'Stand aside.' He reversed his gun, lowered it and fired twice in rapid succession at the lock of the door. The wood and metal shattered under the smashing impact of the bullets. Kicking at the door with his boot, he knocked it in and motioned one of his men forward, covering him with his gun. The man moved into the office cautiously, gun ready, then yelled quickly.

Marsden rushed in close on his heels, stared around him at the office. At first he could see nothing out of order, except for that fact that Simon was nowhere to be seen. Then he moved over to the desk and saw the pair of legs protruding from behind it. Kneeling quickly, he turned the lawyer over onto his back, lifted his head for a moment, then let it fall with a snort of anger and disgust.

'This must be some of that marshal's doin',' he snarled viciously. 'Get him. If it's the last thing we do, we've got to find him now. Those deeds that were in the safe. He must have got 'em.' He turned and jerked his head towards Silvers. 'Mount up the rest of the boys, scour the town from one end to the other. I don't care how many of the townfolk you've got to get out of their beds, but I want every place searched, and properly this time. He's slipped through our fingers once too often.'

'You figger he's still in town, boss? Maybe he decided to try and make a run for it.'

'If he did, he won't get very far,' muttered Marsden grimly. 'He'll be a fool if he tries to. No, he's still in town somewhere. Besides, we've found his mount and that *hombre* at the livery stables knows better than to give a horse to anybody tonight.'

He waited until the men had piled out of the office, then pulled the lawyer's body out into the middle of the room, went over to the table and picked up the jug of water, carrying it back and throwing it over the other's face.

For a moment nothing happened, then the other spluttered, coughed and twisted his head to one side.

'All right,' ground Marsden. 'What happened here tonight? It was that marshal, wasn't it?'

The other stared at him for a long moment, not comprehending. Then he seemed to collect his senses for he tried to get to his feet, failed, and sank back onto the floor again, shaking the water that ran from his forehead into his eyes, onto the floor, holding on to the desk nearby with one hand to steady himself or he would have fallen again.

'Get on your feet, damn you,' snarled Marsden, 'and tell me what happened. That goddamned marshal is still somewhere on the loose in town. But my men will find him, never fear. Right now, I want to know if he took anythin'.'

The lawyer licked his lips, then nodded, putting up a hand to his head as a spasm of pain lanced through it. 'He forced me to open the safe and give him those title deeds. The ones you had made out when you took over the other ranches some years ago.'

'So. Then he's just signed his own death warrant.' For a tense moment, the lines of his face deepened as he pursed his lips into a hard, thin line. He looked over the lawyer deliberately as the other struggled to his feet, but made no effort to help him. Screwing up his eyes, Simon staggered to his desk and sank down into his chair, reaching into his drawer and pulling out a flask of whiskey which he gulped down, coughing as the sharp liquor hit the back of his throat. He wiped the back of his hand over his mouth.

'I thought you said you'd have that marshal pinned down

124

before sunset,' he growled. 'Instead of that, he manages to get in here and holds me at gunpoint without your men doing anything to stop him.'

'Somebody in town must've been hidin' him,' snapped the other. 'Now shut up while I try to think this out.' The lawyer was silent for a while as the other paced up and down the room, his hands clasped tightly behind his back. Then Simon said harshly: 'I don't see why you're so worried about those title deeds. He can't do anything with them even now that he's got them. There's nothing there that could incriminate either of us in a court of law.'

Marsden spun on him, his face suffused with a flush of anger. 'You talk like a fool at times, Simon,' he said tersely. 'Why do you figger he took 'em if he didn't have some plan how to use 'em? What happens if he manages to dig out one of those men we forced to sign the deeds?'

'That isn't likely. Most of 'em pulled out and headed back East at the time. You know that as well as I do. Besides, that was all so many years ago that there won't be any left in this territory.'

'You're makin' one hell of an assumption,' growled the other, not convinced, 'If you're wrong, it could be the finish for us. Until we've got Enders and those deeds, we can't be safe.'

The other moaned as he clutched at his head, poured himself another shot of whiskey. He gulped it down and grimaced, then pushed himself onto his feet, shaking his head a little as he attempted to clear it. 'You want me to come with you?' he asked finally. 'I can get a gun and—'

'You stay right here,' roared Marsden angrily. 'You've caused me enough trouble this night already. He isn't likely to head back here but I'll leave a man nearby if it makes you feel any better.'

Steve crossed an open patch of ground, padding in silence over the smooth rocks, reached a small clump of cottonwood and crouched down among them, listening to the faint sounds of the night, the creaking of the branches in the high wind that swept along the trail at this point, the rustle of grass bending in front of the gale; and the small, scraping of hoofs on the smooth rocks. He crept forward, coming downslope into the boulders along the trail. A man laughed hoarsely and Steve halted abruptly. He had almost blundered into their midst. They were less than three yards away, two of them, seated in the lee of a small ridge, sheltering as best they could from the biting wind. The harsh laughter shivered along Steve's spine and he felt his flesh squirm and contract with a sudden chill.

Steve crept a little to one side, keeping them both in sight. The wind congealed the sweat that had popped out on his body. He was so close to them that he could almost reach out and touch them and yet they were not aware of his presence there. It would be the simplest thing in the world to pull his gun and shoot them both down, and neither man would know what had hit him.

But he had no direct quarrel with either of these two men, even though he knew they would shoot him down on sight if they spotted him. He eased himself forward, sinking to the ground as he reached a rock that overhung the trail, almost immediately above them as they squatted on the ground, talking between themselves, their voices raised to be heard above the thin, banshee wail of the wind. Then, without warning, a stone moved under his feet, tore away from the rock and went rattling off down the slope.

'What was that'?' muttered one of the men, starting to his feet, drawing his gun in a swift, lithe movement.

'Huh?' grunted the other, barely glancing up.

'I'm sure I heard somethin'. Close by, too.'

'You're just gettin' jumpy,' growled the other, moving back a little and pulling the collar of his mackinaw higher around his neck, trying to get as much warmth out of it as he could.

Steve crouched against the rock, trying to make himself as small and unobtrusive as possible. The wind caught at his clothing and whipped it around his body and the blood drummed through his veins and behind his forehead until he thought the rapid, loud beating of his heart against the ribs must surely be heard by the men. He heard the first man moving around, caught the metallic clatter of his gun on the rocks as he edged below him,

'I tell you I heard somethin'.' The gruff voice came from almost directly beneath the spot where he lay, holding his breath until it hurt in his chest. 'Could be that jasper of a marshal tryin' to head out of town and get back into the hills. If he wanted to do that he'd have come this way.'

'Don't talk foolish,' muttered his companion. 'They'll have run him to earth by now. He'll have been shot down and Marsden and the others will be celebratin' in town. We ought to be there now, instead of sittin' out here in this wind. There's a storm blowin' up and I'd feel a heap better if I had some whiskey and food inside me.'

'Maybe that *hombre* managed to slip through 'em.' The other was still not convinced. 'I'm goin' to take a look, anyway.'

'Suit yourself.'

There was silence, followed by the stealthy rustle of a man edging his way along the trail so as to get out into the open. Steve risked a slow lift of his head, told himself tightly that he should have shot down both men when he had had the chance. The feeling against violence, against shooting down men without giving them an even chance, was beginning to get him into a lot of trouble. Sooner or later, if he wanted to stay alive, he would have to adopt the ways of these men, mean and cunning and vicious. Shoot first and talk later.

He saw the man move out of the shelter of the tall rock and begin to slip forward, caught the faint metallic gleam of the drawn gun in his right hand. The other's progress was clumsy and slow in the teeth of the wind which had risen to gale force now and was howling at the other as he tried to move forward without exposing himself too much. Then the other paused, looked about him as if sniffing the wind. He stood there for a long moment, bracing himself against the numbing force of the wind, turned to go back, then paused. He uttered a harsh yell of warning as he caught a glimpse of Steve's body lying on the rock, whipped up his gun and fired. The shot was instinctive, the action purely reflex and the bullet struck a few inches wide of Steve's position, Before the man could fire again, the Colt in his hand spoke and the man suddenly clutched at his chest, seemed to teeter on his heels for a long moment before clinging to the rock trail wall for support, his legs giving under him as he sank to his knees. His gun went off again, but the bullet ricocheted off the trail a couple of inches in front of him as he toppled forward, hitting his head with a sickening sound on the rocks, a sound that carried easily in spite of the wind.

Swiftly, knowing that he had little time, Steve swung on the second man. The other had risen to his feet and was staring into the darkness, trying to pick him out, his gun half drawn from its holster when Steve fired. The man tilted drunkenly sideways, pawed at the air for a moment, then dropped beside his companion.

Without pausing to ascertain whether there were any other men watching this trail, Steve ran back over the treacherous rocks to his mount, swung up into the saddle, and put his horse down the tricky stretch of ground onto the trail, heading towards the hills.

It was after morning before he finally rode down from the mountains and onto the plains which stretched between them and Anderson. But instead of taking the trail into town, he headed for the Gantry ranch. For what he had in mind, he needed help and Gantry was the man he reckoned would be able to provide it.

There was smoke curling from the chimney of the ranch-house as he rode into the courtyard and slid wearily from the saddle. A couple of the hired hands came out of the nearby bunkhouse and one moved over, took his horse from him, and led it to the trough at the side of the house before taking it into the corral.

Vic Gantry came out onto the porch with Beth close at his heels. He stumbled a little on the top step and Gantry caught at him, helped him into the house.

'You look all in,' said the rancher, concernedly. 'We never expected to see you again. The news was that Marsden had every man he could get out in the hills lookin' for you. Then there's a posse goin' around, tryin' to find your trail, just in case you decided to double back out of the hills.'

Steve shook his head, 'They tried to stop me leavin' Chester,' he said tiredly, sinking back into the chair, eyes half closed with fatigue.

'Chester!' There was a mute inquiry in the other's gruff tone. 'Then you did manage to get through?'

'Sure, I got through, just ahead of Marsden and his boys. I talked with Ed Simon, the lawyer, but he wouldn't admit to anythin' when I first saw him.'

'Just like I said,' muttered the rancher grimly. He seated himself in the other chair, then turned to the girl. 'Get somethin' to eat for Steve,' he said. 'He must be hungry, ridin' all night like that. When did you last eat?'

'I don't rightly remember.' It was difficult to keep his eyes from going together and he made himself a smoke to keep both hands and mind occupied. From the kitchen, he heard the girl getting a meal ready and a few moments later, the smell of frying bacon sharpened his mouth. He lit the smoke, but got little pleasure from it, his mouth and throat too dry to be able to appreciate it. But it kept him awake, drove a little of the weariness from his mind.

'What happened after Marsden rode into Chester?' queried the other.

'The lawyer fella warned him I'd been and they posted men on all of the trails out of town and the others began searchin' for me. I managed to hide out in one of the abandoned storehouses for the day and then paid another call on the lawyer, but this time, I went unannounced and with a gun ready. I forced him to give me those title deeds.'

The other's eyes lit up at that and he leaned forward, suddenly deeply interested, 'So you've got 'em,' he said tautly. 'What do we do with 'em now?'

'I only wish I knew. Unless Marsden breaks and does somethin' foolish, there isn't much we can do with 'em, unless you know of any of those ranchers who might still be in the territory. They could give evidence against Marsden and this crooked lawyer.'

The other sat back, long face drooping a little at that. He sucked in his cheeks in concentration. 'Never heard of any who might still be around. Those who were still alive, headed back East. There was nothin' for 'em to stay around these parts for.'

'Surely they didn't all pull out.'

'Afraid so.' The other's brow furrowed in thought. He lifted a fist and closed it and made a sudden sharp movement. 'Wait a minute, though. There was one of 'em who stayed around for a while. Then he went off prospectin' in the hills.'

'You know if he's still there?'

'Could be. Use to head this way when he rode into town for supplies. A strange man, Abe Travis. It was what Marsden did that started it. Everyone was hurt, but those who cut their losses, sold out at gunpoint and then went back east had a new life to start. But Abe's hurt went deeper than that. He wasn't married, but there was a girl back East somewhere waitin' for him to send for her once he'd got really started. He never did send for her, never went back. I think he was balanced on the edge of bitterness, that one; it needed only a little push to make an outlaw of him, to

130

destroy his faith in all of his fellow men and so destroy himself, to make a bad one out of him. But he didn't go that way. Instead, he went off into the hills alone, shut himself away from everyone. He had a shack up there and an old mine working.'

'And you reckon that Marsden may know where he is, that he's still alive?'

'Doubt it. But there's no doubt that his foreman, Silvers, knows. Once took a heap of gold dust off him at poker in the saloon. Tried to trail him back to the mine, but Abe was a trifle too smart for him, I reckon, for he never did find it.'

'But if Marsden gets it into his head that we can bring this man down to give evidence against him, he'll do all he can to stop him from talkin'!'

'You mean that Silvers will talk?'

'It stands to reason that he will. Marsden will know that without someone to back up our statements about these deeds, they're worthless to us. He'll reckon that I must have had a reason for stealin' them and that reason could only be because I know of somebody who can testify against him.'

'Then we'll have to get on up to Abe's shack as fast as we can,' declared the other. 'Marsden ain't goin' to waste any time once he hears about him. Even if it ain't likely that Abe can testify against him, he'll have to make certain.'

'You know where it is?' asked Steve pointedly.

Gantry shook his head. 'It could be anywhere up in those hills. Abe was always mighty secretive since he discovered that strike of his. Not that it was a rich vein, but you know what these cussed old prospectors are like.'

Beth came in with the meal and set it on the small table. She smiled warmly at him. 'Better eat up before you do any more talking,' she said softly. 'You look as though you could do with a good sleep. Why'd you keep him talking like this, dad?' She turned almost accusingly on her father.

'My fault, Beth. But this is important.' Gantry drew his heavy brows down over his eyes. 'We've got Marsden on the run, but we reckon he'll head up into the hills and try to prise out old Abe Travis.'

Beth looked puzzled for a moment, then nodded. 'I remember him,' she said slowly. 'Didn't something happen to his ranch, and he went off into the hills prospecting for gold.'

'That's right.' Her father nodded affirmatively. 'He's the only one left of the ranchers that Marsden forced off the range. If that killer should hear of him and realise that he can be brought into town to testify against him, he'll be ridin' out there now to shut his mouth for good.'

'But how will you find him in time?' The full implications of this had not been lost on the girl. 'Nobody knows where his shack is and there are almost fifty miles of those mountains and foothills. We couldn't comb them all, especially not with Marsden's men riding them too.'

'It's our only chance,' Steve declared. He glanced at Gantry. 'How many men can you muster right away?' He took his chair at the table, sat down to the heaped plate of bacon, eggs and fried potatoes, trying to control the sudden urgency in him. By now, Marsden would know of the two dead men along the trail out of town, would know that everything could fall around his ears within a short space of time unless he did some fast thinking and fast acting. It would not take long to get his men together and ride out of Chester. It was doubtful though if he would get enough fresh horses for all of his men and it seemed likely that it might take them a little time to ride that trail through the mountains with tired horses.

The girl seated herself at the table, poured coffee and sipped it slowly, keeping her eyes on him, her look grave and serious. 'I'll ride out with you, when you go,' she said quietly. 'I know those hills better than most, used to spend most of my time in them before I went East.'

'No, Beth,' broke in Gantry tightly. 'There'll be shootin' once we meet up with the Marsden crowd.'

132

'I can handle a rifle as well as any man you've got in the outfit,' said the girl quietly. There was no boast in her tone and Steve, remembering how she had used that gun when the stage had been held up, knew that she was speaking the plain, unvarnished truth.

He saw her eyes turn to him, with a mute question in them, but he shook his head very slowly, 'No, Beth,' he said softly, but with an air of finality that brooked no argument. 'I'm not doubting what you've said, but there will be danger and trouble in the hills. We're probably outnumbered by Marsden's men and every one of them is a professional gunman, a trained killer. Besides, there may also be the sheriff's posse from Anderson on our tail. You'd best stay here.'

Her lips parted to make some further protest, then she closed them again and shrugged.

'You have any idea where Abe Travis might be?' asked Steve slowly, as she got up to take the coffee pot back into the kitchen. 'You must know plenty of places where he obviously isn't shacked up, and that could save us a lot of trouble.'

'From what I've heard, he must pan most of his gold in one of the streams up yonder,' said Vic Gantry musingly. 'That ought to narrow things down a bit.'

'He isn't anywhere along the two streams that come down from the hills along the trail just out of town,' said the girl positively, pausing in the doorway. 'I know them both all the way to their source.'

'Then we'll have to ride further along the trail,' said Gantry heavily. He got to his feet, looked down at Steve. 'You feel like comin' with us?'

'Sure. I mean to be in at the end of this chore,' nodded the other. He finished the coffee in his cup, wiped his lips, then stood up, stretching a little. Outside, sunlight had reached the ranch as the sun lifted. The light rolled over the plain like a yellow river, driving the darkness in front of it, touched the cluster of pines on top of the low rise to the east, then came sweeping down the side of the meadow until it reached the courtyard and the corral, softening the contours of the ground as it erased the darker shadows, making everything look more homely, breaking the dullness of the buildings around the wide dirt courtyard. Already, several of the men were going about their morning chores, but Gantry went outside onto the porch, called to one of the men, obviously the foreman, and spoke hurriedly to him in a low undertone. The other nodded tersely, went off to the rest of the men, spoke with them, then vanished inside the bunkhouse.

When they came out, the other men moved over to the corral, got their mounts ready, throwing blankets over them, then putting on the saddles, tightening the cinches.

Fifteen minutes later, they were all set to move out. Steve still carried the title deeds in his pocket as he moved to the doorway, but acting on impulse he turned, took them out and handed them over to the girl. 'Better put these away in a safe place,' he said, speaking casually. 'Marsden will be wantin' to get his hands on them again and it's best that they stay here instead of ridin' out with me.'

There was a momentary look of alarm on her face as the implication behind his words struck her, but she took the packet of papers, held them tightly in hand, fingers curled around them, looking down at the faded yellowish papers with the scrawled signatures on them, as if trying to find some of the answers there to a lot of the questions which were obviously troubling her. Then she said in a voice so soft that he could barely make out the words.

'Take care of yourself, Steve.'

He nodded, forced a quick grin, then placed his hand under her chin, lifting her face, forcing her to look at him, seeing something in her eyes that he had never noticed before. He saw her round, stilled features and the smooth slope of her shoulders, even under the dress she wore, the shining colour of her hair, He thought he saw her lips trembling a little as he pulled her towards him, looking down at her face as it came up. It was like a burst of sunheat in him as he kissed her, felt her respond to him, then draw back.

Vic Gantry called from the yard. 'We're ready to move out when you are, Steve.'

'I'll be right with you,' he called back. He stood for another moment, looking down at the girl, then gently he curled her fingers around the papers, said gently: 'Take good care of them, Beth, and whatever you do, don't hand them over to anybody, especially not to the sheriff. You understand?'

She nodded, her eyes moist. Then she stepped back into the parlour as he turned, strode out onto she porch and stepped down into the dusty courtyard. His own mount was saddled and waiting for him. Swiftly, he swung up into the saddle, pulled the horse's head around and rode out beside Gantry. At the edge of the corral, before they rode onto the wide, dust-covered trail that led up through the meadow, he turned and threw a quick glance over his shoulder.

Beth Gantry was standing just inside the doorway where he had left her, watching them ride out. She lifted a hand for a moment. Then they had swung around a sharp bend in the trail, were moving up the lee of the hills. A few moments later, they topped the rise, moved down towards the distant hills.

As they rode, the heat of the day rode with them. Dust lifted under the feet of their horses. swirled about them in a choking, flesh-stinging cloud. Worse than the discomfort it brought, it also picked them out from a great distance, and Steve knew, as did most of the men, that they could be seen from the mountains still ten miles or so distant.

He rode alongside the grim-faced Gantry, letting his mount pick its own pace to suit that of the others. Thirty men rode with them, but that was possibly only about half the number that Marsden had at his call. The only advantage they possessed was that Marsden might be forced to split his men in order to search for this crazy prospector who seemed to be their only hope of finishing Marsden. As he rode, he wondered whether or not they were jumping ahead of themselves, whether Marsden did know of this man and the threat he might be to him.

At that moment, Marsden was some fifteen miles away to the west, having ridden out of Chester an hour before dawn, rounding up his men as soon as he heard of the shooting of the two men watching the trail from town back into the hills. He had guessed at once that Steve would ride direct to Gantry's in the hope of getting men to follow him, but that was not the only problem on Marsden's mind,

Reaching a fork in the trail, where one winding track led down in a steep plummeting blur to the plain far below, and the other wound up into the higher reaches of the mountains, Marsden reined his mount, signalled to the rest of the party to halt. He motioned the big foreman towards him. Silvers rode forward and halted alongside the rancher.

'You sure about that crazy *hombre* living up here in the hills somewhere?' he grated.

Silvers nodded. 'Sure, I'm sure,' he said. 'Used to bring in gold dust every six months or so. Won plenty of it from him at poker one time in Anderson.'

'How can you be so sure he's one of the men we ran out of the territory?' demanded the other hoarsely.

'His name's Abe Travis. Used to own the Double V ranch until you moved in and forced him to sign it over to you.' Silvers grinned viciously. 'After burnin' down a couple of barns and rustlin' off half his herd.'

'Travis.' Marsden spoke the word musingly. He could just recall it, a name from the past which he had never expected would come back to haunt him. He had felt certain that every man who could have testified against him had either been killed or had left the territory. Now there was this one who could wreck all of his plans and it was clear that somehow Enders knew of him, otherwise he would not have gone to such lengths to get his hands on those deeds. He clenched his teeth in impotent rage. He'd be damned if a crazy prospector was going to stand in his way now. And that interfering marshal would have to be stopped before he caused more trouble. But there was no sense in rushing blindly into this situation. It had to be thought out carefully. He must try to put himself into Ender's mind, to try to guess at his intentions. There was no doubt that once he reached Gantry's place, he would try to get all of the men together and ride out into the hills looking for this man Travis, hoping to bring him in and get him to testify. From what he had heard, nobody knew where Travis was shacked up and the mountains were a pretty big slice of land. It would mean they would have to ride every trail in the hills before they managed to locate the old coot.

In the meantime, the Gantry place would be virtually undefended, with probably only the girl there and—

The girl! The thought came to him in a single flash of understanding. He whirled in his saddle, facing Silvers. 'Take most of the boys with you and try to locate this prospector. Bring him in to me – alive if possible.'

'What are you goin' to do, boss?' asked the other.

'I'm taking half a dozen of the boys and ridin' down to Gantry's place. I figger it ought to be almost undefended now. If I can get my hands on the girl, I might also get my hands on those title deeds. Giving Enders some credit for sense, I doubt if he'll carry them with him into the hills while he goes lookin' for Travis. That would be a stupid thing to do. My guess is that he's left 'em at the ranch with the Gantry girl.'

Silvers nodded slowly, the spark of understanding in his eyes. 'Makes sense,' he agreed reluctantly.

'Sure it makes sense. It's the only thing he can do. With the girl and the deeds in my hands, I've got the whip hand over them all. They'll be only to ready to do what I ask. This could be the answer to everything.' He slammed one fist into the palm of his other hand. 'Now ride! Search every likely place. That crazy old fool has got to be somewhere. And remember, try to bring him in alive.' There was a look of malicious anticipation on the rancher's broad features. He signalled to half a dozen of the men to remain with him, then waited until the rest of the boys had gone off along the hill trail, before putting his mount to the steep downgrade.

The tall crests lifted all about them, as Steve and the others rode up into them. Cloud touched the topmost peaks, masking them from view, but they lifted more than a thousand feet above the trail, uprearing pinnacles of stone which had been there for countless millions of years and seemed ageless and eternal compared with the puny men who rode the lower slopes. They crossed the first two creeks and moved on without giving them a second glance. Steve felt a momentary pang of uneasiness as they forded the second creek, water swirling about his ankles as his mount plunged forward through the spuming foam that ran around the jagged, upthrusting rocks a little distance upstream. Had the girl been right when she had said that Travis's place was not along either of these two creeks? If she were wrong, they would be wasting valuable and precious time ignoring them.

He put the thought brusquely out of his mind. The feeling of tension in him continued to grow, forcing a way through the weariness that was in his body and mind. Half an hour later, they reached a point where a deep stream flowed swiftly down the upper reaches of the hills. It ran fast and came down through a deep wrinkle in the rock, but there was a narrow, half-seen trail that led up through stunted bushes until it vanished over the lip of a ledge higher up. Steve reined his mount, signalling a halt. Sliding from the saddle, he bent and examined the ground here quickly. There was some sign there although the rain had washed a lot of it away.

'This track has been used quite recently,' he said positively. 'It could be that Travis has his shack up there.' Gantry lifted his head, peered up, shading his eyes from the strong glare of the sunlight reflected from the smooth rocks. 'Won't be easy gettin' up there,' he muttered through clenched teeth. 'He'll use a burro. That's nothin' more than a pack track.'

'Seems the logical place,' murmured one of the men, nodding. 'Seems I remember hearin' about this trail. Old Indian track that leads up over the mountains through one of the passes. Used to be the Old Starr Mine somewhere along here.'

'How're we goin' to get up?' persisted Gantry. He scanned the area for any other track alongside the stream, but there was only a mass of tumbled rocks on the far bank, impossible to take even a burro through them.

'If this is the place, then we have to get up,' said Steve quickly. He put his mount forward, leaning over its neck to enable it to get a better grip on the treacherous ground underfoot. Straining upward, the bay fought its way over the rough ground, pushing through the thorn bushes that barred the way. Steve felt them catch and drag at his clothing, raking across his arms and legs, but he ignored them, gritting his teeth, urging the horse forward as it threatened to slip back down the trail. The water flowed swiftly past him, filling his ears with the sound and the dampness of it came to him in the hot, still air.

At the top of the ledge, the trail widened, although it was still broken in places. He turned in the saddle, motioned the rest of the men up, edged forward a little as they began the steep climb. It was slow progress. More than half an hour fled before the last man clambered up onto the ledge, and they were ready to move forward along the bank of the stream.

They had been on the slow ascent up into the hills when Steve paused, held up his hand for silence.

'What is it?' asked Gantry tautly.

'Thought I picked out running horses.' Steve listened again, but this time he heard nothing, He shook his head a little wonderingly, worried. Either it had been his imagination, or a freak echo had brought that brief moment of sound down to him. He felt sure that it had originated somewhere directly ahead of them, though possibly on the other side of the stream which was their landmark now. The dull, muted thunder had come and then faded equally swiftly.

Then, a moment later, the sound came again, and this time there was no mistaking it. A large party of men, Steve decided, listening carefully, assessing the sound, trying to determine its direction. And the only large group of men who would be riding the hills apart from this party, would be Marsden's men, moving in from the west.

He walked his mount along the trail, the faint prickling along the small hairs on his scalp giving mute warning to him. Trouble lay ahead, but how close and from which direction, he wasn't quite certain. He eased the guns slowly in their holsters. There were more tag-ends of sound lifting on the still air, but they were reflected from the rocks, making it impossible to judge their true direction.

Halfway along a steep-sided canyon that opened up in the rocks, they caught the first, distant break of gunfire, shots making little sounds in the air above them. The firing stayed brisk as they urged their horses forward, not sudden crashing volleys of sound.

'Trouble,' said Gantry shortly. He pointed along the trail. 'It's coming from up there, about half a mile away.'

'You figger those are Marsden's men and they've located this fellow?'

'Seems the only explanation to me,' nodded the other, his face grim. He loosened the Winchester in its saddle scabbard. 'Reckon we'd better ride or we'll be too late.'

They put their mounts to a quick, brisk, gallop. Here the walls of the canyon held them in, keeping them to the narrow trail where it was only possible for two men to ride side by side. Out-thrusting bushes grew from patches of soil on the rocky walls of the canyon, scraping across their heads and shoulders as they forced their way through. The sun beat down through the hazy dust, trapped inside the canyon, beating at their bodies.

Then the canyon wall dropped down on either side, they moved out into open, rock-strewn country, with the trail running on levelly in front of them. Less than four hundred yards away, it ran straight between two huge boulders, with the stream rushing alongside the trail itself. The sound of firing came from beyond the boulders.

'We'd better dismount and move in on foot,' said Gantry practically. 'On horseback, we'd not have any room to manoeuvre.'

It made sense, agreed Steve mentally. He slid from the saddle on the run, continued to move forward even after he had released his hold on the reins, both guns out, looking back at the men as they rushed forward into position. They moved in on the narrow gap between the boulders, gunfire in their ears.

CHAPTER VII

GUN HARVEST

As he edged forward, Steve got his first view of the cabin and the old mine workings. They stood in the centre of the wide open ground which lay beyond the rocks. He could understand now why nobody had found Abe's hiding place before now. The other had come up here to be away from everyone else, a man caught in a web of bitterness that had twisted him in on himself, driving him away from his fellow men. But he had also found the yellow metal here, either inside the old mine that was supposed to have been worked out many years before, or in the stream that came rushing out of the side of the mountain, just on the far side of the clearing. The shack itself had been built hard against the solid rock wall of the mountain, and this meant that anyone attacking the place could only do so from the front. There was no way at all of getting at Abe Travis from the rear.

Marsden's men were spread out among the rocks, entirely surrounding the small plateau, rifle and revolver fire pouring into the wooden shack. Steve could see the splinters of wood flying from the walls of the building where the bullets struck home. It was difficult to make out any of the attackers. They were evidently crouched down out of sight behind the boulders, keeping their heads well down.

142

An occasional shot came from the direction of the shack, indicating that Travis was still alive, still resisting this attack.

'We take 'em from the rear?' muttered Gantry softly. His eyes glittered brilliantly as he turned to Steve.

The marshal gave a quick nod, glanced up at the rocky wall in front of them. 'It would be better if we could get up there,' he said, pointing.

'Not much chance of that,' grunted the other. 'Too steep for quick climbing and Travis won't be able to hold much longer in the face of that fire.'

Even as he spoke, a harsh voice from the rocks called loudly: 'Better come on out, Travis. We've got you surrounded. You can't get out.'

A pause, then a voice yelled thinly, defiantly, from the shack: 'You won't take me, you buzzards. I can shoot down any one of you who shows his face. And I've got plenty of food and water here which you ain't. I reckon after you've fried out there in the sun for a while you'll change your mind about who's got the upper hand.'

'Damn you, you crazy old coot,' roared the voice again, and Steve recognised it as belonging to Silvers, Marsden's foreman. Evidently he was in charge of the men here. If that was the case, then where was Marsden? Why wasn't he here in at the kill, making certain that the menace which faced him no longer existed. The feeling of uneasiness in his mind suddenly crystallised into something far more urgent. He gripped the guns more tightly in his fists, then edged forward, motioning the rest of the men to move up with him. They had to flush these killers out of the rocks – and fast. He had the feeling that Marsden was still one jump ahead of him and there was the impression of inexorable time urging him to a new decision.

Out of the corner of his eye, he saw a head lift from among the rocks less than ten yards away. Swiftly, he swung his guns on it, both weapons roaring at the same time. The man uttered a shrill, sharp yell and fell back, body bouncing down the rocks as he was hurled off balance by the impact of the slugs.

'Better give up like the man says, Silvers,' Steve called harshly. 'Or we'll nail all of you.'

There was a loud curse from the foreman as he lay hidden among the rocks. Then he gave a loud shout.

'That's this interferin' marshal, boys. Seems he's brung the Gantry bunch with him. Here's our chance to kill two birds with one shot.'

Bullets hammered close to Steve as he pulled himself back behind the rocks. For the time being, the gunmen had forgotten the man hiding in the shack as they turned to face this new menace at their backs. But Gantry's men were well hidden, keeping down out of sight, firing only when they saw a movement in the rocks ahead of them. Steve drew in a deep breath, held it in his lungs for a long moment, letting his gaze wander slowly and carefully over the tumbled rocks and boulders around the shack. For a long moment there was no movement there at all.

Then, at the edge of his vision, he saw the two figures that were slowly easing their way forward through the rocks, wriggling snakelike in their attempt to close in on the opening without being seen. His lips curled back tightly over his teeth as he waited for them to approach a narrow, open stretch of ground where they would have to advance without cover. As he anticipated, they waited among the rocks for several moments, then began to crawl forward over the narrow fissure. He waited deliberately, until they were halfway across, then sighted carefully, dropped both of them before they had a chance to get back under cover.

There was no compunction now in his mind against killing these men. Most of them were almost certainly wanted outlaws who had joined up with Marsden, doing his bidding in return for shelter and pay. The return fire was savage and immediate. It hammered about him, bullets thudding into the dirt and ricocheting off the hard rocks, screeching past him with the high-pitched yell of tortured metal.

Every muscle in his body was tight. Lead flailed through the air from every direction. A man dropped groaning behind one of the rocks nearby and he crawled over to him, went down on one knee beside him, saw the red stain on his shirt where the slug had hit him in the shoulder. Tearing off a strip of material from the man's shirt, he plugged the wound, then thrust the other back against the rock.

'Lie there until this is finished, and then we'll get you back to a doctor,' he said quietly. 'It's only a flesh wound but you'll lose plenty of blood if you try to move around. Keep still and you'll be all right.'

The man nodded weakly, closed his teeth with a snap as pain lanced through his shoulder. Steve crawled to the edge of the rocks, risked a quick look around. Silvers was trying to rally his men for a final rush on their positions. Steve could hear the other's bull-like voice raised above the clatter of gunfire, urging his men forward. Crouching down, Steve checked that every chamber of his Colts was filled, then waited. If the others came rushing in they would have to make every slug count if they were to beat them off. Turning his head, he glimpsed Vic Gantry lying full length behind a boulder a short distance away. The other had evidently heard Silvers' shout, knew what it portended, for he too was checking his guns, reloading them.

For several moments, there was a taut, uneasy silence in the narrow valley. Then a solitary shot came from the cabin near the rocky wall, a hundred feet away. One of Marsden's men, edging forward into the open, suddenly yelled and slithered lifelessly down the rocks. Almost as if that solitary shot had been a pre-arranged signal, the gunmen came in, clambering over the rocks, firing as they came, some yelling fiercely, others moving in silently.

Steve sighted on a tall, cruel-faced man who rose up silently from the rocks less than ten feet away. The man spotted him in almost the same instant, pulled up his gun and fired. The slug struck the rock close to Steve's head, sent hard splinters of stone into his face, half-blinding him. But his shot went home. The man's gun dropped clattering onto the rocks. For several seconds, he hung there, his body folding slowly. Then he jack-knifed abruptly and fell to his knees before rolling out of sight between two upthrusting boulders.

Vic Gantry was firing steadily at the men who appeared at intervals among the rocks. Steve cast about him for any sign of Silvers, searching for the big foreman, knowing that so long as the other was alive, he would keep these men moving forward, in their attempt to wipe out himself and the rest of the men. But for a long while, he could not see the other.

Cautiously, he moved deeper into the rocks. The sound of firing was all about him now, the booming echoes from the rocks adding to the din, swelling the sound until it became an inhuman roar. A man rose up from close beside him, clambered onto one of the flat rocks, commenced firing, without seeing Steve lying there. Before he could turn, Steve had shot him down, the man crashing onto the ground near his legs. There was a look of stunned surprise on the gunman's face as though, even in death, he could not believe that he had been hit.

Slowly, the volume of fire was diminishing. One side was gaining the upper hand, but at the moment there was no way for him to tell which it was. Silvers had staked everything on that last wild rush, sending his men forward in an almost fanatical charge through the rocks, as though realising the precariousness of his position. But where was Silvers? Why hadn't the other shown up?

Gently, he squirmed forward between two rocks, feeling the hot touch of the hard stone on his body. Most of the firing was behind him now and he guessed he was moving in the direction of the wooden shack. Then, without warning, before he realised his danger, he heard the hard voice to one side say: 'That's far enough, Marshal. Just hold it there and call off your men or I put a slug into you.'

Very carefully, Steve glanced up, saw that the other had been aware of his movement all the time, that he had been lying in wait for him, waiting until he got close enough before making his move. The gun in the other's hand was rock steady, pointed at his body. There was no chance to try to steady himself and draw from that position with any hope of beating the other, although for a moment the thought lived in his mind, must have shown through onto his face for Silvers drew his lips back in a taut grin and said softly: 'Just make a play, Marshal. I'll really enjoy putting a slug into you. That way, we'll know you're dead. You've slipped through our fingers once too often.'

Steve stared up into the round black hole of the gun, saw the triumphant grin on the man's face, saw his finger tighten on the trigger. His mind seemed very clear, very sharp at that moment as he tensed himself to the sudden impact of lead striking his body, ploughing through flesh and bone, knew that if he was to make any move to save his life he would have to make it now, knowing even as the thought flashed across his mind that it would be no use, that the other had the drop on him, could kill him before he had the chance even to throw himself to one side and bring up his own gun.

The sudden bark of gunfire made him flinch. A little shiver went through him and several agonising seconds passed before he realised that he was still alive, still untouched, and that Silvers was swaying in front of him, striving to hold the life in his eyes, his mouth sagging open. A trickle of blood spilled from his trembling lips as he stood there. With the last ounce of strength in his body he strove to lift the gun in his hand, to line it up on Steve's chest again and pull the trigger, but Steve did not even make any move to twist to one side, or lift his own weapon. One glance at the foreman's face was enough to tell him he would never succeed in his attempt. He was dead on his feet but where had the bullet come from that had killed him in the nick of time?

Slowly, Steve got to his feet, staring around him, then looked down at the foreman's body lying wedged between two rocks. There was a widening stain on the back of his tunic where he had been shot in the back. Lifting his eyes, Steve glanced in the direction of the wooden shack. The door had opened and a man had stepped out into the clearing, a rifle held in his hands. He came forward, a tall, straight man, bearded, with narrowed eyes that still held a bitterness in them which nothing could erase. He moved up to Silvers' body, turned him over with one foot.

'You know who these men are?' he asked thinly. 'They rode up and tried to shoot their way in. Figgered they was after my gold. Now I ain't so sure.'

Steve forced air out of his lungs. 'Wasn't your gold they were after,' he said harshly. 'You're Abe Travis, aren't you?'

'That's right.' The other squinted up at him. 'But if it weren't the gold, then why did they come ridin' here with guns?'

'These are Cal Marsden's men,' said Steve simply. He grew aware at that moment that all firing had stopped behind him. Glancing back, he noticed Gantry striding forward, grim-faced, while the rest of his men rose up from the rocks.

'Marsden!' There was a tightly-controlled anger in Travis' tone. He gripped the stock of the rifle more tightly, almost convulsively. 'So that explains it.'

'They knew that you could help us put Marsden and his men behind bars, if not have 'em strung up,' Steve told him. 'I got hold of those title deeds that Marsden forced you and the other ranchers to sign when he took over some years ago. But we needed someone who could testify as to how Marsden got hold of 'em; and you're the only man in the territory who can do that. I figger that he made you sign them at gunpoint after attacking your ranches.'

He saw the expression that gusted over the other's face, knew then that he had been right in his supposition.

'Where is Marsden now?' grated the other harshly.

'I figgered he'd be here with his men, making sure that they eliminated you,' Steve told him. 'Seems I was wrong and that's what's been worryin' me. If he ain't here then he's at your place, Vic.' He turned to Gantry as the other came clambering over the rocks to them.

'But Beth's there alone.' The other's face blanched at the news. 'If Marsden is there he can—'

'Can you get your men to bring Travis here with them while we ride on?'

'Sure.' Gantry turned, gave orders to his men. 'Let's go.'

They ran along the narrow gulley, leapt into the saddles and put their mounts at the narrow, winding trail that dipped out of the hills, down along the banks of the swift-running stream.

They reached the margins of timber an hour later, swung sharply towards the ranch. As he rode, Steve felt the sudden anger begin to ride him, overriding every other emotion. He cursed himself for not foreseeing that this might happen, for not having considered what Marsden was likely to do in the circumstances. The other had had more men than he needed to take care of Travis when his men found him and it only made sense that he would ride out to Gantry's ranch, figuring that if they were bent on the same thing as his own men, it would inevitably mean leaving the ranch virtually undefended. He had thought himself smart leaving those deeds back there with the girl. Now, he realised how he made a trap for himself. With the girl, Marsden would get the deeds and without them, who would ever believe the testimony of a man everyone firmly believed to be crazy, driven mad with bitterness at losing out when he tried to make a go of it all those years before and a man who, into the bargain, held nothing but hatred for Marsden.

They spurred their mounts at a cruel, heart-straining pace, caring little for the horses so long as they reached the ranch as quickly as possible, perhaps in time to head off Marsden and the men he undoubtedly had with him, although Steve had the unshakable feeling that they could never do this. The other must have had too big a start on them.

At the top of the timber strewn hill which overlooked the meadows, they reined up their mounts for a moment, staring down into the valley, at the cluster of buildings nestling around the spring at the bottom. Smoke still lifted from the chimney and there seemed to be nothing out of order down there that they could see from that distance. Then Steve's sharp glance caught sight of the object that lay in the court-yard a little distance from the steps of the porch and his heart quickened in his chest.

Spurring his horse forward, he rode madly down the grassy slope with Gantry close on his heels. Dust lifted about him as he rode into the courtyard a couple of minutes later. Sliding from the saddle, he ran across the courtyard to the man who lay face downwards on the dirt, arms outflung, legs twisted up under him. He turned the other over, noticed the stain on his shirt, felt for the pulse, but could detect none. Gantry rode up, just as he straightened.

'He's dead,' he murmured dully. 'Shot in the chest. Never had a chance to pull a gun in his own defence.'

The rancher pointed at the marks of horses in the dust. 'Looks like there have been six or seven riders here,' he said shortly. Dismounting, he ran towards the house, calling urgently: 'Beth! You in there?'

There was no answer from the house and anticipating a possible trap, Steve ran forward, caught the older man's arm in a restraining grip before he could clamber up onto the porch.

'Steady,' he said urgently. 'It may be a trap. If they're still in there, they'll shoot you down as soon as you go through the doorway.'

The other tried to shake off Steve's hand, then paused, breathing heavily, as though he had just run a long race, nodded his head bleakly. With drawn guns, they made their way inside. The whole place seemed to have been ransacked. The table was overturned and drawers had been pulled from the bureau, everything in them ripped out, hanging over the furniture, piled in heaps on the floor.

'They must have taken her with them,' Steve said hopelessly. 'And that means they have the title deeds as well.'

'I'll kill Marsden when I get him,' said Gantry. He seemed almost beside himself. Steve could understand the other's feelings. He felt the biting anger, the utter hopelessness within him, knew that they had to do something, everything in him urging him to action, but where had her captors taken the girl? Straight to Marsden's ranch? It seemed the most likely place. Once he was holed up there, it might take an army of men to prise him loose, even though most of his force had been smashed back there in the mountains. Yet because it was the obvious place, Steve was inclined to dismiss it. The only other place was into town. But that too, seemed unlikely. The townsfolk might be all on Marsden's side over the shooting of Carew, the banker, ready to turn on Steve; but when it came to abducting Beth Gantry against her will, that was a different matter.

All in all, he reckoned that Marsden would head back to his own place, intent on keeping the girl a prisoner there until Gantry flowed to his will and agreed to sell out, and until Steve was handed over to him. He glanced swiftly at the man beside him, wondering if any of these ideas had occurred to him, but there was nothing on the other's mask-like features to indicate what kind of thoughts were running through his mind at that moment.

'I figger that he's headed for his own place right now,'

Steve said thinly. 'He can't have much of a start on us. He must have had some trouble tryin' to find those deeds and judgin' from the mess here Beth put up quite a fight.'

'Once he gets to his ranch, we'll never get him out,' said the other bleakly.

'Then is there any trail we can take that'll bring us out ahead of him?'

'There's the trail across the mesa, but it ain't ever used now. Scarcely any trail there at all.'

'Then we've got no choice,' Steve said coldly. 'We'll need a couple of fresh horses and the sooner we start out, the better.'

Leaving the house, they made their way to the corral. There was a small group of horses at the far side and in less than five minutes, they had a couple roped and saddled and were riding swiftly out past the bunkhouse, along the meadow, then swinging north as they reached the trail at the top of the low hill. As they rode, pushing their mounts to the limit, the country grew rougher, full of mesquite and scrub. They left the grasslands behind, headed out into the white alkali of the desert.

Here, the high noon sun beat down on them with a brassy glare, making it impossible to look up at the mirror-like heavens, and even to glance at the ground sent stabs of pain lancing through their temples into their brains as the harsh brilliance shocked back at them from the alkali dust. Within minutes of entering the Badlands, the dust lifted around them, churned up by the pounding hoofs of their mounts, following them like a swarm of flies, getting into their nostrils and forming a burning mask on their faces. Sweat mingled with the dust until every pore seemed filled with it, itching and painful. Steve rubbed the back of his hand across his face, but even that slight movement seemed to tear at his flesh, leaving it raw and painful.

He narrowed his eyes to slits, pulled his bandanna across the lower half of his face, trying to breathe through the cloth, using it as a filter for the dust, but although that eased things a little, there was no way of escaping the tremendous waves of heat that were refracted from the alkali, as it shimmered and writhed all about them. There was no doubting why this trail was scarcely ever used. A man would have to be a fool to ride this trail in preference to that further to the south which, although rocky, ran through more pleasant country.

The minutes dragged. The faint outline of hills on the far edge of the desert land seemed as far away as ever. Perhaps it was an illusion, thought Steve dully, but it even seemed to be receding from them, as though determined they would never reach it.

Not once, in that wild, terrible ride over the alkali flats did they ease up the cruel pace they had set on leaving the ranch. They rode without stopping, intent only on one thing; to get between Marsden and his ranch, to swing around and cut in ahead of him. Unless they did that, then everything they had done would be in vain. The men who had died so that Abe Travis might came in and give his testimony, would have died in vain. Marsden would once again be the supreme boss of this territory, undisputed king of the land and no one would dare to stand against him; and because of that, progress here might be held up for a generation or longer. Steve did not want to think what must be happening to Beth Gantry at that moment, wherever she was.

Cal Marsden rode tensely, his rifle across the saddle in front of him, his eyes raking every inch of the trail ahead and above and to the sides. Not that he expected trouble here but until he got the girl back to his own place, he would not feel safe and secure. There was no telling what had happened back there in the hills, though it was clear that things were going the way he had expected. Gantry and that marshal had ridden out with most of their men, leaving only the girl and a couple of hired hands at the ranch. If they bumped into Silvers and the rest of the boys, there would be a showdown up there and he still felt a little unsure as to the outcome of it. That marshal was fast – there was no doubting that and in spite of the fact that he reckoned Silvers had more men with him, other things might even up the sides a little.

He slewed his eyes in the direction of the girl. She was sitting in the saddle, with her hands tied to the saddle-horn in front of her. It was not comfortable but he was taking no chances with her. At the moment, she was his passport to safety. So long as he had her, Gantry would do everything he told him to, even to handing over that marshal to him, and agreeing to his terms for the sale of his ranch. Then, he would have become the only rancher in the territory, would have wiped out all of the opposition. Everything would be his as far as the eye could see to the west of Anderson. It sent a little glow of pleasure through him as he turned the thought over in his mind, savouring it. But it also made him more wary. He could not allow anything to go wrong now. That marshal seemed to have the ability to turn up when he was not wanted, when he was least expected, and if Silvers and the others had been defeated, then once they realised he was not riding with that bunch, they would figure out almost at once what had happened, what he had done, and would head back for Gantry's place. Once there, it would not take long for them to realise he had the girl and where he was taking her.

'Don't you reckon we ought to make better time, boss?' growled one of the men thinly. 'I don't like the idea of being caught along this particular stretch of the trail by a man like that marshal if he's still alive.'

'There's too heavy timber here,' Marsden opined. 'Good cover for any man lyin' in wait for us.'

'Hell, you don't reckon they're ahead of us, do you?' grunted the other in surprise.

Marsden snapped his head up, looked around, and glared at the other. 'I never underestimate a man like Enders. He's mean and he's smart. We know he may have reached the Gantry place if he's still alive. He won't have wasted any time once he finds I'm not there.'

'Mebbe not,' agreed the other. 'But he's no magician. He can't fly.'

'He won't be far behind,' broke in the girl quickly. She lifted her head and stared from one man to the other. 'You'll not get away from them. No matter where you try to hide.'

'That's where you're wrong,' said Marsden harshly. 'So long as we have you, I reckon your father is goin' to do everything I tell him. He's got no choice if he wants to see you alive. And the first thing he'll do is hand over Enders to me. The next will be to sell out his ranch and move out of the territory. I figger I can offer him a fair price for it.'

One of the men snickered. They rode on through the tall pines that lifted sheer to the sunlit heavens, with the sunlight flashes glancing through the trees into their eyes. Beth tried to loosen the bonds that tied her hands to the saddle-horn, but they had been tied too well and she only managed to chafe the flesh of her wrists without loosening the ropes even by a fraction.

They came out of the timber for a little while, the trail stretching away in front of them through a stretch of more open ground. Giving a quick glance about him, Marsden motioned the men out into the open, blinking as the strong sunlight struck his face with an almost physical blow. To their left, off in the distance, there was the white, shining strip of the desert.

The ride across the final stretch of the desert was the worst. Here, where there was a trail, it was little more than a narrow, winding ribbon of ground that had been trodden down by horses and by men a little more than the rest of the ground. In places, they came across boulder-fields where they were forced to dismount and lead the horses. It might have been possible to ride a horse through them but it would have needed care and patience. They might have had the care at that moment, but they didn't have the time to be properly careful and a lame horse would mean the end of their try to swing ahead of Marsden.

They came to a ledge, climbed over it and found themselves staring along the trail where it wound away into the distance. There was no sign of Marsden and the others and Steve felt the tightness grow in his chest, saw Gantry eyeing him inquiringly.

'I don't know,' he said, guessing at the other's thoughts. He felt uneasy. 'They could have made better time than we fingered and be past this point by now.'

'If they are, then we'll never catch 'em or take 'em by surprise.' The bleakness was back in the other's eyes and voice. He fingered the rifle in its scabbard.

'We'll have to take the chance that they haven't reached this place yet.' With an effort, Steve made the decision. 'Get the horses out of sight and we'll wait for 'em to show.'

The other made as if to protest, then shrugged, took the reins of the two horses and led them away, deeper into the bush. He came back a few moments later, carrying the Winchester. Steve pointed to a slight rise of ground from where they would be able to see for some distance along the trail, and where thick bushes grew out of the hard, stony soil, giving them plenty of cover.

As he squatted in the thick, tangled bushes, Steve felt anxious to tangle with Marsden. It seemed strange that until only a little while ago he had never met this man whose fate seemed to be intricately entangled with his own, had known of him only from a signature scrawled at the bottom of a letter asking for his help in arresting a suspected killer and robber. Now he knew that if there was one man in the world he wanted to kill, it was Cal Marsden. It was strange the tricks fate played on men, he mused, letting his eyes wander over the white scar of the trail as far as he could see, to the point where it vanished into the distant trees. A man answered a letter, thought that it would mean only a small episode in his life, something easily forgotten once it was over, only to find that a whole new vista had opened out for him, arousing the deepest emotions of which men were capable.

He thought again of the girl, visualised the sheen of her hair where it flowed over her shoulders, the look in her eyes and the quiet note of her voice as he had last seen her. The thought drove all else from his mind but the deep-seated anger that threatened to overwhelm him completely. He forced himself to control it, aware that he needed a clear mind now, more than ever before. Marsden was a clever and implacable enemy, would do anything in his power to keep what he had already gained, even stopping at nothing. Certainly murder seemed to be nothing new to him and the girl's life would mean nothing if anything went wrong with their plan.

'There they are.' Gantry's sharp whisper shocked his mind back to the present.

He stared out into the sun-drenched distance, saw the small group of riders come into view from the trees. He felt himself tighten. Gently, he eased the Colts from their holsters. He reckoned there were half a dozen men riding with Marsden and they would have the girl somewhere in the middle of them so that there was no chance for her to escape by riding off the trail. That was going to make things difficult, to get at the men without risking the life of the girl. It only needed one stray bullet and her life could be forfeit.

As the riders came nearer, it was obvious that they were wary and already suspicious, riding more slowly than necessary, eyes swivelling to watch every inch of the trail, casting ahead of them for trouble. One man riding in the lead, he recognised him a moment later as Cal Marsden, had a rifle across the saddle in front of him.'

'This ain't goin' to be easy,' whispered Gantry. 'They're alert for trouble and they've got Beth in the middle of 'em.'

'If we can pick off Marsden, I reckon the others might scatter,' said Steve tightly. 'Think you can pick him off with the Winchester?'

'I'll try,' grunted the other. He steadied himself and aimed the rifle at the oncoming group. It was not going to be easy for him, Steve reflected, shooting at Marsden with his own daughter riding close behind him and he wondered if he ought to have taken the rifle and done it himself. But almost at once, the rifle cracked sharply.

He saw the man in the lead suddenly whirl, clutch at his shoulder, dropping the rifle. There was a harsh shout. Then the men with him had slid from their saddles and were running for cover. Steve opened up with the Colts, thumbing the hammers back in rapid succession. It was almost as though he was not even pausing to take proper aim, but four of the men, running from the trail, suddenly dropped and lay still. The remaining two hesitated, then ran back to their mounts, climbed up into the saddle and turned, racing back along the trail in the direction from which they had come.

Swiftly, Steve lunged to his feet, moved out into the open. Marsden was still in the saddle. He whirled as he saw Steve running towards him, pulled the gun from its holster with his good hand and threw a couple of badly-aimed shots at the other. Then, wheeling his mount savagely, he rode it alongside the girl's, clutched her around the middle, and pulled her down. They hit the ground in a tangled heap while Steve was still more than fifty yards from them. With a savage movement, Marsden still retained his grip on the girl, heaved her to her feet and backed away with her along the trail, holding her in front of him like a shield.

'Come one step further and I'll put a bullet in the girl,' he roared at the top of his voice.

Beth struggled furiously, but her strength was no match

158

for Marsden's. Steve slithered to a halt, knowing that he would not be able to fire at Marsden without hitting the girl.

'That's better,' shouted the other. 'You're not quite as clever as you figgered. I suppose you managed to get hold of Abe Travis. You must have or you wouldn't be here. But it won't do you any good. I'm goin' to shoot you down right now. And as for Gantry, once I catch up with him, he'll be finished too.'

'That's where you're wrong, Marsden.' Without warning, Gantry's voice came from behind Steve and a little to one side. Marsden had not known that the other had been there, crouched in the bushes. Gantry had not shown himself after firing that first shot from the Winchester. Now he had somehow made his way to the side of the trail.

Marsden started at the sudden interruption, whirled instinctively, trying to bring the gun to bear on the rancher and in that same moment, as he was off balance, Beth Gantry thrust herself free of the other's grip, ran for a couple of paces and then stumbled and fell. Swiftly, Steve brought up his gun, triggered it savagely, saw Marsden teeter on his feet as the slugs tore into his body. He arched his back, clutched at himself, jerked and shuddered, falling forward.

When the gunsmoke cleared, he was lying face-downward on the rocks beside the trail, his gun still clutched tightly in his right hand, his finger on the trigger he had never pulled.

Steve went forward, helped the girl to her feet. She sucked in a deep breath as he pulled a knife from his belt and cut the ropes which bound her wrists. The skin had been rubbed red raw, he noticed. Then she was in his arms as he tightened them around her slender waist.

'I knew you'd manage to find me,' she said quietly. 'Is he dead?'

Vic Gantry came forward, nodded. 'He's dead all right,' he said throatily. 'I reckon we can forget about those other two men. They won't stop ridin' until they're out of the territory now that Marsden is dead.'

'Once we get Travis into town, we'll soon settle things with Sheriff Blaine, too,' said Steve grimly. 'I reckon they'll lock him up in his own jail to await trial.'

'Could be that we'll be needin' a new sheriff when that happens,' said Beth quietly, meaningly. 'A man we can trust.' The way she said it struck him powerfully and the pressure of her fingers entwined in his told him a lot more than mere words what was in her mind.